Henry Bagg Smith

Celebration on Greenfield Hill

Henry Bagg Smith

Celebration on Greenfield Hill

ISBN/EAN: 9783337327132

Printed in Europe, USA, Canada, Australia, Japan

Cover: Foto ©Andreas Hilbeck / pixelio.de

More available books at **www.hansebooks.com**

Celebration on Greenfield Hill.

Address of Welcome
—by—
DEACON N. B. HILL,
reply by
REV. GEORGE W. BANKS.

Historical Discourse

DELIVERED AT THE

One Hundred and Fiftieth Anniversary of the
Formation of Greenfield Church,

MAY 18, 1876,

BY

Rev. H. B. Smith,

PASTOR OF THE CHURCH.

Commemorative Address

OF THE LIFE AND CHARACTER OF THE

REV. DR. TIMOTHY DWIGHT,

FOURTH PASTOR OF THE CHURCH AND PRESIDENT OF YALE COLLEGE,

—by—

REV. PROF. TIMOTHY DWIGHT, D. D.

CHRONICLE PRINT:
SOUTHPORT, CONNECTICUT.
1876.

Greenfield, Ct., May 19, 1876.

Rev. H. B. Smith,

Dear Sir:

Having listened to your able, interesting and truly valuable historical discourse, and believing it should be preserved, and the valuable information it contains be placed within reach of every family in the parish, we respectfully request a copy for publication.

NATHANIEL B. HILL,
JOSEPH DONALDSON,
W. O. MURWIN,
JOHN BURR,
JOHN MURWIN,
JOSEPH BETTS.

Greenfield, Ct., May 25, 1876.

Messrs. Deacon N. B. HILL, Deacon JOSEPH DONALDSON, W. O. MURWIN, JOHN BURR, JOHN MURWIN and JOSEPH BETTS,

Gentlemen:

Your communication has been received requesting a copy of the historical discourse, delivered May 18th, for publication. I am thankful that it meets your approval, and trusting to your judgment, I submit the discourse to you, though prepared amid a pressure of pastoral labors.

Yours truly,

H. B. SMITH.

THE CELEBRATION

OF THE

ᎾNE ᎻUNDRED AND ᎬIFTIETH ᎪNNIVERSARY

OF

GREENFIELD CHURCH.

MAY 18TH, 1876.

THE people, notwithstanding the rain, assembled from far
and near in large numbers to celebrate the one hundred and
fiftieth anniversary of the organization of the Congregational
Church on Greenfield Hill. Natives of the place, descendants
of former residents, citizens of adjoining towns, and from the
cities of New York, New Haven, Bridgeport and Norwalk,
ministers, lawyers, physicians and teachers filled the church to
its utmost limits. The benevolent hands of the ladies of the
parish had adorned the church and the pulpit with wreaths
and flowers, which were much admired.

On account of the sickness of Hon. Abram Wakeman, of New
York City, Judge Thomas Bradford Dwight, of Philadelphia,
was called to take the chair and act as president of the day.
After a few pleasant remarks from Judge Dwight, he called
upon the choir to sing a hymn in the old tune of "Majesty."
Then the congregation were led in an appropriate prayer by
the Rev. Marcus Burr, of Rockville Centre, Long Island, N. Y.,
at the conclusion of which the choir, in an admirable manner,
sang another old tune to the words, "Before Jehovah's awful
throne." Next a cordial welcome was given to all the invited
guests by Deacon N. B. Hill, which was gracefully responded
to by the Rev. George W. Banks, of Guilford, Conn. Then the
choir sang another hymn to the tune of "Northfield." The
historical discourse herewith published, giving an account
of the settlement of the town of Fairfield, and the parish

of Greenfield, with the history of the church, was then delivered by the pastor. The morning services were concluded by the singing of "Auld Lang Syne." Then the numerous guests, together with the whole congregation, were invited to a bountiful collation, provided by the ladies of Greenfield, in the basement of the church.

Having done justice to this repast, the people reassembled in the sanctuary, where the afternoon services were commenced with the singing of an anthem by the choir, after which Prof. Dwight, of Yale College, gave a most discriminating and admirable address concerning the life and character of President Dwight, the fourth pastor of Greenfield Church. Then followed brief addresses from the neighboring pastors and others. Eloquent responses were given to the following sentiments:

"Our Mother, the Mother of Churches," by Rev. Dr. E. E. Rankin, of Fairfield.

"Our Elder Sister," by Rev. G. J. Relyea, of Green's Farms.

"Our Younger Sister," by Rev. G. E. Hill, of Southport.

"Our Youngest Sister," by Rev. H. W. Pope, of Black Rock.

"Our Oldest Daughter," by Rev. Mr. Dudley, of Easton.

To the sentiment of "Greenfield Hill," the Rev. R. G. Hibbarb, a former pastor, responded. Professor Thomas A. Thatcher, LL. D., presented the congratulations of Yale College, and recommended the refounding of the old academy on a sure basis under the honored name of Dwight Academy. Rev. Dr. Rogers, of New York City, being called upon, gracefully presented the salutations of the oldest church on Manhattan Island, the original church of "New Amsterdam," at the Battery. After the singing of the "Easter Anthem" by the choir, and the doxology, the president of the day made a few parting remarks, and the public services were brought to a close with the benediction by the pastor. As if to assure us that all is well, the sun came out at the close of the meeting and gladdened the hearts of all as they returned to their several homes, cheered with the sweet remembrance of a most enjoyable anniversary.

ADDRESS OF WELCOME.

By Deacon N. B. HILL.

————◆•◆————

Mr. Chairman, Ladies and Gentlemen :

In behalf of the people of Greenfield, I welcome you to Greenfield Hill, to unite with us in celebrating upon this centennial year the 150th birthday of this church. We make no apology for this celebration, for it has ever been the custom, among the nations of both ancient and modern times, to commemorate by suitable manifestations of public gratitude events of great importance. The formation of a church here upon this hill was an event of great importance. Though small in its beginnings it has been great in its results, and we look forward to still greater results in the future. Yes, our forefathers did a great work here one hundred and fifty years ago, and we have assembled upon this occasion to view the work of their hands, to go about this our Zion, " to tell her towers, mark well her bulwarks, that we may tell it to the generations following." We would call our thoughts from the busy present and the ever glorious prospective future and fix them upon the past, reflecting upon all the way which the Lord our God has led us on. To you who once lived here and have wandered away, we welcome you back to the old home to-day; and to you whose fathers or mothers, or grandfathers and grandmothers once lived here, we welcome you back to the home of your fathers. May this day be such an inspiration to you all, that when you shall have had enough of wandering up and down in the earth, or when you shall have acquired enough of its riches, its honors and its glory, you will bring those riches, honor and glory back to this old Greenfield Hill, and here in the home of your fathers enjoy that happiness and find that rest which you will probably find nowhere else. Again, ladies and gentlemen, one and all, I bid you welcome, thrice welcome.

RESPONSE TO THE ADDRESS OF WELCOME.

By Rev. G. W. BANKS, of Guilford, Ct.

Mr. Chairman and Friends:

I have been asked by the Committee of Arrangements to respond in a few words to the very kind and generous address of welcome which has just been made by Deacon Hill; to respond on behalf of the natives and former residents of this parish, who have found homes in other places, but who have come back to-day to mingle with you in the festivities of this anniversary.

I scarcely think, however, that I am the proper person for this service; so frequent have been my visits during the seventeen years since I left home, that I feel more like one of the people here, and can hardly express the feelings of those who have been for many years absent, and perhaps this day have returned for the first time.

However, I think I can say, with those for whom I speak, that we are not ashamed of our native place. We have wandered off into other towns and distant parts of the State, into other States and distant parts of the Union, and wherever we have met with strangers, who have asked where we came from, and have answered them, almost universally, if they were people of intelligence, they have replied, " Oh ! yes ; Greenfield Hill ! that was where Dr. Dwight went from to the presidency of Yale College ! Was it not ?"

Such character and fame has that good and great man given to this place ! We are proud of the natural attractions of this place, and the unsurpassed scenery from this beautiful hill. We are proud of the honorable history of this ancient church, and as we shall to-day, led by its pastor, refresh our minds with the facts of that history, and as we shall have our attention called by my honored instructor at old Yale to the character of Dr. Dwight, and the influence he exerted upon his times, we shall go away from this feast of rich things with a higher estimate than ever before of the place that gave us birth. No, sir, we are not ashamed of our native place.

Perhaps it is a little immodest for us to say, and yet you will pardon us for saying it, that we have mainly tried to live and act so that the old parish should not be ashamed of us. We have carried out into the various communities where our lot in life has been cast, and into the various employments and professions in which we are engaged, the principles and truths that we have learned in this House of God, or in others that stood upon this site, and these same principles and truths we are trying to live up to, and to inculcate in other places; to put upon other minds the same impress that here was put upon ours. I presume it is safe to say, sir, that the large majority of those of us who have thus gone out, and who are still living, received our training and instruction in these principles from one honored teacher (Rev. Thomas B. Sturgis). Some of us can say, what very few can say in these days of frequent ministerial changes, that we never had but one pastor. And I can assure you, sir, that to such, it is by no means the smallest part of the pleasure of this joyous occasion, that we are privileged as we come back to welcome that beloved pastor to his native land and to this field of his life's labors; to see his face once more, to take his hand, and, I trust, before the day is over, to hear, as of old, his familiar voice in this place. We count it no small privilege that by him we learned how to think, and think consecutively, and more than that, to think with reference to our relations to God and to our fellow men, that by his hand our feet were guided into wisdom's ways. And we wish to assure him that the seed which for more than a quarter of a century (more than one sixth part of the entire history of this church) he so faithfully sowed broadcast over this field, is yet bringing forth fruit, not only here but in other and distant communities.

But, sir, the joy of our coming back is tinged with sadness, as we miss from the places that so long knew them, men who were honored and exerted a wide influence for good here—such men as Judge Hill, Gov. Tomlinson, Capt. Baldwin, Doctor Blakeman, and many others who might be mentioned. To some, probably, who have come back and who used to know every person in the parish, there are but very few familiar faces in this audience; and we are all reminded of the old yet ever forcible words of Scripture, "One generation passeth away and another cometh."

Nevertheless, the fact that calls us together to-day is a glorious one, viz., that the Church abideth. Like some great training school, the generations one after another pass through it into the beyond. For one hundred and fifty years it has held its place on this beautiful hill, like some perennial fountain, sending forth streams that make glad the city of our God.

And we believe that for generations yet unborn it shall be what it has been in the past; that till time shall end the sound of the church going bell shall be heard sweetly echoing over these hills and valleys—

> "And here thy name, O God of Love,
> Our children's children shall adore,
> 'Till these eternal hills remove
> And spring adorns the earth no more."

Most heartily, therefore, Mr. Moderator, do we accept the generous welcome that has been extended to us. We shall enjoy the day and its services, and long remember them. This will be a red letter day in our histories, and when at its close we go down from this "Hill of Zion" to our homes and our work again, we will go with the words of the Psalmist in our hearts—"Peace be within thy walls, O! Jerusalem, and prosperity within thy palaces." "For our brethren and companions' sake, we will say peace be within thee."

THE HISTORICAL SERMON.

By Rev. HENRY B. SMITH.

REMEMBER THE DAYS OF OLD, CONSIDER THE YEARS OF MANY GENERATIONS: ASK THY FATHER AND HE WILL SHOW THEE, THY ELDERS AND THEY WILL TELL THEE.—*Deuteronomy* xxxii, 7.

By this divinely inspired precept we are commanded to keep in mind the history of the past, and call to remembrance the days of our forefathers. In so doing we shall consider the years of many generations. Since the first settlement of this old town of Fairfield eight or ten generations of men have lived, performed their several parts and passed onward. Also, six or seven generations have inhabited the hills and vales of the parish of Greenfield since the organization of the church, all of whom, excepting the present, have been gathered to their fathers. As we review their history, we are reminded that one generation goeth and another cometh in rapid succession. Does not filial obligation require us to recall their noble deeds and to keep them in remembrance? If the voice of God did not call us to the performance of this duty, filial affection should constrain us to perform the obligation we owe to a pious and noble ancestry. Never should the honorable names of Banks, Burr, Bradley, Hill, Hull, Wakeman, Sherwood, Baldwin, Nichols, Meeker, Jennings, Morehouse, Betts, Ogden, Wheeler, Wilson, Perry and Bulckley be allowed to pass into oblivion. The families bearing these names have chiefly composed the inhabitants of North-West Parish from the origin of its settlement until now. In all the towns and parishes of my acquaintance, I know not any where so many have lived and died in the place of their nativity from generation to generation.

The inhabitants have married and intermarried to such an extent that each family bears some relationship to every other in the community. But as the blood has been good, and the origin noble, well may it be perpetuated. A distinguished authority, Dr. Dwight, declares: "That the people of Connecticut

are descended from ancestors distinguished for their wisdom
and virtue, and owe, under God, to this fact, the prominent
features of their character and the great mass of their blessings;
and no New Englander can read the history of his town or
State without rejoicing that God has caused him to spring from
the loins of such ancestors." As the first settlers of North-West
Parish belonged for more than eighty years to the old parish of
Fairfield, we shall first allude to the history of the town of Fairfield, before considering the history of the society and church of
Greenfield. For we claim partnership in all the honors, prosperi-
ties and adversities through which Fairfield has passed in its remarkable history. Thankful I am that so many descendants are
present to-day from far and near, to rekindle their affection for
their ancestral homes and to pay homage to their pious, patriotic and noble progenitors. I am sorry, however, that the early
records of Fairfield were destroyed by fire in the American
Revolution, and that the records of Greenfield Church and Society are so imperfect and incomplete. But I have done what
I could with the imperfect materials at my command, and with
the knowledge within my reach.*

In common with all the old towns of New England, the first
settlement of the town of Fairfield was about 237 years ago,
nineteen years after the landing of the Pilgrim Fathers on
Plymouth Rock. In this early period the English colonists were
greatly excited and disturbed by a warlike and roving tribe of
Indians—the Pequots—who roamed about to kill and destroy.
The colonists on the Connecticut River suffered such a loss
of life and property that they were constrained, for the sake of
protection, to war against them. On the 13th of July, 1637, a
decisive battle was fought, the English colonists being victo-
rious. A portion of the Pequots, pursued by Captain John
Mason and his soldiers, fled west of the Connecticut River by
a circuitous route to Sasco Swamp, near Southport, where they
were secreted by a small tribe of Indians called Unquowas.
Here the small army under Captain Mason exterminated or
scattered these savages on that memorable day which delivered
the colonists of Western Massachusetts and Connecticut from
fear of evil. Hon. Roger Ludlow, who accompanied Captain
Mason with the troops in pursuit of the Pequots to Sasco
Swamp, was so much pleased with the beauty and fertility of
the land that he projected the scheme of a settlement. Accord-

ingly, the following year, 1638, he, with some eight or ten other families, removed from Windsor, Conn., to Unquowa, now called Fairfield.

Mr. Ludlow was Deputy Governor of Connecticut for several years, and the principal planter. Very soon his small colony was joined by other families from Concord and Watertown, Mass., and soon became numerous enough to form themselves into a distinct township. Then this whole section of country was, to a great extent a wilderness, where dwelt wild beasts and roving savages. Much praise is due to Mr. Ludlow for the part he took in the settlement of Connecticut and of the town of Fairfield, since he was the most distinguished lawyer of the colonies, and assisted in the construction of the first written constitution originated in the new world—one which was the type of all that came after, even of the Republic itself.

He made the first purchase of the land from the Indians, included in the town of Fairfield, which originally embraced all the territory lying between Stratford and Norwalk, and extending six miles back from Long Island Sound. At a later period the town purchased of the Indians all the land six miles farther north, including most of the territory now embraced in Fairfield, Easton, Weston, part of Westport, and Bridgeport. The whole six miles, including all the northern section of the old town of Fairfield, as far north as Reading Centre, was purchased of the Indians for thirty pounds. Then the town voted to distribute nearly all the common unoccupied land to the individual citizens. This distribution of the land made the long lots, as they were called, and they were deeded to the settlers in width according to each one's assessment in the list of estates, in length, as far as they chose up into the wilderness. Some of the division lines of these long lots at length became roads on which the people travelled, and extended up into the uninhabited country as far as Reading Centre. Some of these roads have been used as highways from the laying out of these lots till now. These roads, corresponding to the long lots, ran due north, without any regard to the hills or valleys. It is also evident from the town records that these lots extending up into the wilderness were used as pasture lands by the early settlers. "At a meeting of the proprietors, held January 25th, 1726, it was voted by the major part of said proprietors that there should be a flock of sheep kept in Greenfield Parish for the summer ensuing, and Charles Hill, Moses Diamond, Jr., and Benjamin Banks were appointed sheep masters to take care of the sheep. Voted also that the place to let the sheep should be at the house where the said parish meet on the Sabbath days, and the time to let the said sheep should be Monday and Friday nights." Such sheep masters to take care of the flocks were evidently necessary then to protect the sheep from the ravenous wild beasts, the wolves and bears which roamed over these hills and vales.

Then the town offered rewards for killing wild beasts. For every wolf killed the Selectmen paid 40 shillings; for every old bear 50 shillings; for every cub or young bear 20 shillings. It was further ordered, that whoever killed a wolf in the town, if they expected to be paid for it, must bring the wolf's head to the Town Treasurer, who should keep an account thereof. No wonder, therefore, that the early inhabitants of Fairfield had stockade forts built to protect their families from the ravages of the wild beasts and the more savage Indians. In those times the town kept watch by night and ward by day.

Among the first settlers of Fairfield and North-West Parish was John Banks, a distinguished lawyer and an extensive land holder. He was afterwards chosen representative to the General Court of Connecticut, and appointed to important public offices on the part of the State; a man of excellent character and public spirit, who had the confidence of the Legislature in a remarkable degree. From him all the Banks of this town are supposed to have descended, and his descendants have become almost as numerous and distinguished as were the descendants of Jacob in the land of Canaan; and may their virtues never be less. Of equal celebrity and public spirit was Jehu Burr, one of the pioneers of the North-West Parish. In his day he was much employed in public affairs, on account of his ability and character. He was father of Daniel Burr and grandfather of Rev. Aaron Burr, who became president of Princeton College, New Jersey, and one of the most distinguished preachers of the gospel during the colonial period. From Jehu Burr nearly all the Burrs in this section of country have descended, and most of them have been worthy of their pious and noble ancestry. Another of the early and distinguished citizens of the town of Fairfield was Francis Bradley, who had eight sons and one daughter, most of whom settled in the township. His son,

John Bradley, had nine sons and three daughters, who settled in the North-West Parish, afterwards called Greenfield; from whom have descended some of the most worthy and distinguished citizens of the town of Fairfield and of the commonwealth of Connecticut. If time would allow, I should love to speak of other pioneers of Fairfield, such as Thomas Hill, Samuel Bradley, and many of like celebrity, who, in their day and generation, honored the name and place that gave them birth.

Previous to the American Revolution, Fairfield Town was one of the most wealthy and populous towns in the Connecticut Colony, having, in the year 1756, 4,455 inhabitants. On this account, as well as on account of the superior character of its people, Fairfield exerted a controlling political influence in the State and nation. Since the present is the centennial year of our existence as a Republic, I must allude to the prominent part taken by your forefathers in securing our American independence and our national existence.

Though Connecticut was one of the great producing States during the American Revolution, both of men and money to carry on the war, yet she has never had her full merit recognized in any historical work published, and the same is true of the town of Fairfield, which did more and suffered more, according to her population, than any town in New England.

While Generals Warren and Putnam have become world renowned for their patriotism and heroism, who has ever heard of Captain Ebenezer Banks, who, like General Putnam, left his plough in the field when he heard of the battle of Lexington? Then learning that a public meeting would be held that afternoon on Greenfield Hill, he hastened to the place of concourse. By his exertion, with the aid of others, a company was raised in Greenfield and vicinity and soon started to go the place of conflict. Here is the sword he carried then and through the war, and has upon its hilt inscribed his name, Captain Ebenezer Banks, 1760, showing that he owned and carried this sword sixteen years before the declaration of American Independence. But never have the deeds and sacrifices of that patriotic band of soldiers, nor those of General Silliman of Fairfield, or of Major Chapman of Green's Farms and their troops, been adequately portrayed on the page of history, though they performed an important part in securing the freedom and independence of the United States. During the American Revolution

Fairfield was the most patriotic township in Southern Connecticut, and furnished about the same amount of men and means to carry on the war as New Haven. Hear this testimony to their patriotism :

> "BOSTON, Nov. 24, 1774.

Gentlemen—The testimony which the patriotic inhabitants of the Town of Fairfield have given of their attachment to the common and glorious cause of liberty, by their liberal donation of 750 bushels of grain by Captain Thorp, has afforded much comfort as well as seasonable relief to their friends in Boston, who are now suffering under the cruel rod of ministerial tyranny and oppression. Your obliged friend and humble servant,

> HENRY HILL.

To JONATHAN STURGES and others.

By order of the Com. of Donations."

Here is a curious manuscript, more than one hundred years old, in which are written the names of those men of Fairfield who were summoned, twelve persons each night, to guard the town and act as watchmen from May 24th, 1776, to Feb. 18th, 1777.* On the last page of this pamphlet is this declaration:

"The foregoing persons were legally warned by a lawful warrant from lawful authority.

> Test, DANIEL SHERWOOD,
> *Constable of Fairfield."*

Also the following charge was given to the constable:

> "FAIRFIELD, 9th of June, 1777.

You are desired to deduct from persons noted in this book, who served when warned at the rate of three shillings per night, and to be particularly careful that none be paid who did not serve. Also keep a particular account of every person who neglected going on guard when warned.

By order of the Selectmen.

> Test, THADDEUS BURR,
> *Selectman."*

The patriotic zeal of the men of this town soon became known to the British soldiers, which led them to destroy the village of Fairfield by fire in that memorable month of July, 1779. At that time the English soldiers burned in Fairfield and Green Farms 3 churches, 100 dwelling houses, 77 barns, 19 stores and as many other workshops, and nearly all the buildings in the old town of Fairfield. Greenfield Hill being three miles away, escaped

* *Note B—*Appendix.

the terrible and general conflagration. But of the fear the people suffered, and of the sacrifices they made, in common with their brethren in other parts of the township, no tongue can tell. Still we may now rejoice in their patriotism and suffering, which secured to our State and nation all our social, civil and Christian institutions.

Returning from this digression I must hasten to speak of affairs pertaining more particularly to the North-West Parish, as it was first called. This parish came into being under difficulties, on account of the unwillingness of the Fairfield parish to part with any of its supports. The old society could not bear the thought of losing so many worthy members, and so large a proportion of their wealth and strength. As the people in this part of the town had made the Sabbath day's long journey for generations, the inhabitants of Fairfield supposed that they could travel the same road for many years longer. Consequently, they strongly opposed their petition to the General Court of Connecticut for separate church privileges. Still the people of this section of the town had their hearts set upon it, as the following petition will show:

" TO THE HONORABLE GENERAL ASSEMBLY sitting at Hartford the second Thursday of May, 1725. The humble prayer of the inhabitants of Fairfield North Village humbly sheweth, that there are about fifty-five families living north of Fairfield, at a considerable distance from the town, some five or six miles, and the nearest of them about two miles and a half or more, whose lists amount to £4,000, which inhabitants labor under great difficulties on account of their enjoyment of some of the precious means of grace, especially the proclaiming of the word of life, in the ordinary way and means God uses in the conversion and bringing home poor, lost and undone sinners. Not only ourselves are frequently obliged to be absent from divine worship, but our poor children are under a kind of necessity of perishing for lack of vision, both which are very troublesome to those who are inquiring what they shall do to be saved, and that are hungering and thirsting after Christ and salvation and righteousness in and through him. The distance of the way, especially in bad weather, utterly incapacitates many persons, old and young, to go to the house of God, which makes us willing rather to expend considerable of our earthly treasure in maintaining the public worship of God among ourselves, than to lose our spiritual treasure and undo any of our poor immortal souls, esteeming each of them better than a one thousand worlds.

Hoping and humbly begging and praying that the honorable

gentlemen of the Assembly will pity us, and be nursing fathers to us, and deal with us as they would be dealt with; encouraging of us in our endeavor to honor God and obtain eternal happiness beyond the grave, that they would please to consider there are many places made district societies, the less than we, and nearer the town; as West Haven, Newington, and many others; and also that the town from which we separate is well able to maintain their minister without us, they having without us £13,000 on their list. If the Honorable General Assembly will be pleased to hear this, our prayer, we will ever pray, etc.

Signed by Thomas Hill and sixty other men.*

On consideration had in the lower house this petition was rejected.

Test, THEODORE KIMBERLY,

Clerk."

Very soon after the rejection another petition was presented to the Honorable General Assembly by Thomas Hill and others, asking for a committee to be appointed to view the inhabitants of the parish, and report to the next General Assembly in October, 1775.

Their petition was granted for a committee. That committee, consisting of Messrs. Copp, Lewis and Hawley, reported favorably to the General Assembly in October. "At a General Assembly holden at New Haven, in his Majesty's Colony of Connecticut, in New England, on the 14th day of October, in the 12th year of the reign of our Sovereign Lord George, King of Great Britain, 1725, upon the petition of Thomas Hill, of Fairfield, in behalf of himself and other of his neighbors living within the bounds following: South southwest by rear of the building lots in Fairfield, easterly by the Mill River so called, east north-easterly by the parish of Stratfield, north by the north bounds of Fairfield, first brought to this Assembly, hearing the reasons offered by Mr. Ebenezer Wakeman, agent for the old parish in Fairfield, why said Hill and neighbors should not have parish privileges granted them, as well as the arguments of said petitioners why they should be a parish, do hereby order and grant that said petitioners shall be a parish, and are hereby enabled to set up the worship of God among themselves; and the bounds aforesaid shall be the bounds of said parish, and so remain until this Assembly shall order otherwise. And it is hereby enacted that said parish shall have and be allowed all privileges as are by law allowed to other parishes in this government."

* *Note C*—Appendix.

But the name of the parish was not changed from North-West to Greenfield until two years after, as the following record will show:

"CONNECTICUT COLONY.

At a General Assembly holden at New Haven, in His Majesty's Colony of Connecticut, in New England, on the 12th day of October, in the first year of the reign of our Sovereign Lord George Second, King of Great Britain, 1727. This Assembly orders that the North-West Parish of Fairfield shall be called by the name of Greenfield, and be so recorded."

From this record you will perceive that Greenfield Parish, at its origin, embraced all the north portion of the town of Fairfield. In the year 1757 some families in the north-eastern section of the town of Fairfield were organized into the Baptist Church and Society of Stratfield, and in the year 1757 several families in Greenfield Parish helped form the Congregational Church and Society in Northfield, town of Weston, and in 1763 a large number of families left Greenfield Church and Society and formed the Congregational Church in Weston, now Easton. Since that time the bounds of Greenfield Parish have remained much the same as they were more than one hundred years ago, being four miles square. In Dr. Dwight's day the parish numbered 1,000 inhabitants, and in 1836 about 1,200. Near the close of the last century flax was extensively raised as an article of commerce in Greenfield and Fairfield, even more than in all New England. Theodore Burr told Dr. Dwight that for ten years, when he was naval officer of Fairfield, there was sent out of the town annually an average of 20,000 bushels of flaxseed. Then could be seen here in Greenfield twenty acres of flax in a single field. But long since flax has ceased to be raised as an article of commerce, and onions have taken its place, and many thousand bushels of the latter are now annually raised for the New York market. Few parts of the world are more fruitful and healthy than the parish of Greenfield. "In my own congregation of 1,000 persons," says Dr. Dwight, "during one year of my ministry here, not a single person died, and during another year only two, and one of those was an accidental death." The parish has always been noted for the salubrity of its climate and the beauty of its scenery. Well has the pen of Dr. Dwight embalmed these characteristics of the place in prose and poetry, and made them known wherever the English language is spoken or read. We do not wonder that the muse inspired him to portray in poetry the beautiful scenery from his country seat on Greenfield Hill, for a more enchanting spot cannot be found.

After the removal of Dr. Dwight to New Haven his homestead was purchased by Isaac Bronson, Esq., a gentleman of wealth from New York city, as a summer residence, to which place he retired during a large portion of each year as long as he lived. He greatly improved the place, the parish and the town, by setting out beautiful shade trees. And the same work has been continued by his son, Frederick Bronson, Esq., and by his grandson, who bears his father's name, and is the present owner of the estate.

With the first settlement of the State, town and parish, the cause of education received the early attention of the people. They would not allow their children to grow up in ignorance, but desired them to be educated and qualified to become useful and worthy citizens. Therefore, our forefathers reared the church and the schoolhouse side by side, and led their children to these fountains of human and divine knowledge. Ever since, in the land of the Puritans, the church and the schoolhouse have been the light to enlighten the minds and ennoble the hearts of the people. Nay, they have been the fortresses to defend, and the glory to crown the land of our fathers. In Greenfield, from the first organization of the church and society, the educating of the children and the preaching of the gospel have been regarded of equal importance. At the annual parish meeting provision was made every year for supplying the schools with teachers, and for maintaining the preaching of the gospel. At a meeting held October, 1735, " voted, that there shall be a school kept eleven months in this parish, after this manner: Four months in the centre school; three months in Hull's Farms, and two months in Lyon Farms; and that the county money shall be divided in proportion to the time above mentioned." So the common schools were annually provided for according to law, at the annual meeting of the school society, for more than a century.

When Dr. Dwight settled here a new impulse was given the cause of education, especially the higher education of the children and the youth. Soon after his settlement he started a select school in the southeast room of the dwelling house now owned and occupied by Mrs. Uriah Hubbell. In due time the select school grew into an academy, and a building was erected on the common east of the church, for the Greenfield Academy. The school grew so popular, and became so famous under Dr. Dwight's instruction, that students flocked to it from all parts of the United States, from Canada and from South America. It was Dr. Dwight's ambition to make his first class of pupils equal in scholarship to the students of Yale College, so that the Greenfield Academy almost became a rival to that institution of learning. Many of his scholars, in after years, became celebrated, and distinguished in all the learned professions. After Dr. Dwight, the Rev. Jeremiah Day, D. D., taught the academy for some time, so that Greenfield has really furnished two distinguished presidents for Yale College. Some of the other celebrated teachers of the Academy were Rev. Dr. Samuel Blatchford, Rev. Wm. Belden, Rev. Nathaniel Freeman, Wm. Dwight Waterman, Esq., Charles Shelton, Esq., Park Hill, Esq., and many others. But at length, for the want of a permanent fund, the Academy decreased in numbers, and has for some years ceased to be.

Could a better thing be done, at the one hundred and fiftieth anniversary of Greenfield Church and Society, by some men of wealth and descendants of the fathers of this parish, than to endow the old Academy under the honored name of Dwight Academy, from its distinguished founder ? A word to the wise is sufficient.

I shall now proceed to speak of the meeting houses which have been occupied as places of worship. The first meeting house was built before the parish was formed and the Society established. The building must have been a very cheap and rude structure, still it was used for a house of worship. "At a meeting of the North-West parish it was voted, November 11th, 1725, that the meeting house shall be the place where the parish school shall be kept six months in the year. Also, March 28th, 1726, the parish voted that the house we meet in shall be the place to ordain Rev. John Goodsell. That house was used only temporarily as the place of worship; for at a meeting of the North-West parish, held October 7th, 1726, it was voted that a meeting house should be built, and be begun the year ensuing, and that the dimensions of said meeting house shall be 52 feet in length, 42 feet in breadth and 24 or 25 feet between joints. At the same parish meeting it was voted that the meeting house shall be set and stand half way between Mr. Samuel Whitlock's northeast corner of his home lot and the meeting house where we now meet. Thomas Hill, John Burr, Moses Diamond and Benjamin Banks were chosen a committee to take care of building the meeting house, and to agree with some person or persons to build the said house. The parish voted December 11th, 1727, that Samuel Thorp and Benjamin Darling shall have £5 12s. more than their bargain for framing said meeting house."

" In December, 1730, voted that Lieut. Moses Diamond shall have power to agree with any persons to carry the work on the meeting house, so far as the parish shall raise money for the same, and to be paid for his trouble. In December, 1736, voted that there shall be a pew built on each side of the pulpit at the committee's discretion. The following year, December, 1737, voted that Moses Diamond, Jr., be a committee to lay out what money is raised for the meeting house, and that Samuel Diamond, Jr., and Joseph Banks be a committee to regulate the pewing of the meeting house, and they shall lay out every man his place according to what he has paid toward building the meeting house. In January, 1740, voted that there shall be four braces put in the meeting house, and March, 1742, voted that the meeting house be finished, so far as to lath and plaster under the upper floor and under the gallery floor, and to make one seat around the gallery."

So by degrees the fathers built the house of the Lord; but September, 1743, the parish " voted that those persons who had paid the most toward building the meeting house shall have pews laid out to them in the house, and that every man who has a pew laid out shall be at the charge of building the same." Accordingly, the pews having been built they were accepted, and Joseph Wheeler had pew No. 1; Benjamin Banks, No. 2; Joseph Diamond, No. 3; Nathaniel Hull, No. 4; Daniel Bradley, No. 5; Benjamin Gilbert, No. 6; John Thorp, No. 7; Joseph Banks, No. 8; Samuel Wakeman, No. 9; Daniel Burr, No. 10; John Gilbert, No. 11; Samuel Bradley, No. 12; Benjamin Sherwood, No. 13; heirs of Eliphalet Hull, No. 14; Joseph Hill, No. 15; Jabez Wakeman, No. 16; David Williams, No. 17; Samuel Price, No. 18. In confirmation thereof we have consented to set our hands and seals, this 22d day of September, 1743.

ANDREW BURR,
SAMUEL BURR,
JOSEPH WAKEMAN,
Committee for assigning the seats."

The parish then "voted that Mr. Samuel Bradley shall get a bell for said Greenfield Meeting House, and said bell shall be lodged at the minister's house of said Greenfield." That was the first bell, probably, that was ever rung to call the people together to the house of God on Greenfield Hill, 133 years ago.

Seventeen years after, the second meeting house having become old and dilapidated, the parish "voted, February, 1760, to build a new meeting house, and to have it stand on the place where stands a monument of stones; and that Samuel Bradley, Jr., be a committee to apply to the County Court in behalf of the parish to affix and establish the described place for the meeting house to stand on. Also voted, that the dimensions of the new meeting house shall be 60 feet in length, 42 feet in breadth, and have a good, proportionate well built steeple." In November, 1760, the parish voted "that as many pews as can with convenience be laid out, on the ground floor of the new meeting house, by joiners that understand the business, and the spots or places so laid out, shall be fairly sold to the highest bidder, and the money raised to defray the expense of the house. Also voted that those who purchase the spots or places be obliged to build their pews by a limited time, and to build them uniform, all alike." In the following year the spots for pews were sold, as the record shows:

" We, the subscribers, being appointed at the meeting of the 10th of November last to sell the spots or pews, then voted to be laid out in our new meeting house for pews to be erected on, have, according to the vote of the parish, at their above said meeting relating to said pews, laid out and sold the above said spots or places for pews in the manner following, namely, with the assistance of David Bradley, Jr.: Beginning at the east side of the south double door, have laid out the spots or places for pew No. 1, and so successively laid out and numbered all around the house till we come to the west side of said double door, they being No. 26; and have also this day sold the above spots or places, except pew No. 15, for the purposes aforesaid, to the following persons, with the sum of each spot or place annexed to his name, which persons are obliged by the conditions of said vendue to have their pews well built and completed, upon their own cost or charge, by the first day of October next, or forfeit the same to the Society." Accordingly they were sold as follows : To Gershom Banks, pew No. 1, £14 15s.; to Samuel Bradley, pew No. 2, £16 10s. The whole amount of the sale of these spots or pews was 489 pounds 12 shillings.*

At length the third meeting house being completed—Dr. Dwight's church, as it has been called—"the parish voted, at a meeting held October, 1762, to have the old meeting house and second house of worship pulled down, and Mr. Joseph Hill and Mr. Daniel Sherwood were chosen a committee to order the pulling down of said house, and parcel it out and sell it at public vendue to the highest bidder, in behalf of the parish."

The new house of worship was much admired in its day, on account of its fair proportions and its tall and elegant steeple, the belfry of the church commanding an extensive view of the Long Island Sound and shore. One historian, Mr. Barber, "declares that no other spot in Connecticut can show such a commanding, extensive and beautiful prospect." In his day, from the belfry of Dr. Dwight's church could be seen seventeen churches, five lighthouses, and East Rock, near New Haven. In that meeting house the people of Greenfield worshipped for the long period of eighty-two years. At length, like all other material things, it grew old, and a new meeting house was demanded for the worship of Jehovah. Soon after the settlement of Rev. Mr. Sturges as pastor, the subject of building a new house of worship was talked about and agitated by the people of Greenfield. But how could it be done, when all the pews in the old house were held by deeds derived from their fathers? It was a difficult thing to get the consent of even a majority of the pew owners to give them up, as a step preparatory and necessary to the pulling down of the old meeting house. Still, after much labor on the part of the pastor, Rev. Mr. Sturges, Governor Tomlinson and others, the consent of a majority of the pew holders was obtained to pull down the old and build a new meeting house. The committee of the Society, then consisting of Deacon John Banks, Deacon William B. Morehouse and Mr.

* *Note D—*Appendix.

Samuel Betts, took the responsibility of pulling down the old church. Having done the work of taking it down, a new house of worship must be built. Governor Gideon Tomlinson, Doctor Rufus Blakeman, Deacon William B. Morehouse, Deacon John Banks and Mr. Horace Banks were appointed a committee to superintend the building of the new meeting house.

While all the members of the church and society contributed generously and worked nobly to secure the new Gothic meeting house, special mention should be made of Deacon John Banks and Deacon Wm. B. Morehouse, who were most active in the laborious work of building that most beautiful house of worship, which was much admired, until five years after its erection the house was entirely consumed by fire, Sunday night, November 14th, 1853.

Those persons who had built the Gothic church at great expense, toil and sacrifice, could not help exclaiming, as they saw it in ruins:

"Our holy and beautiful house, where our fathers worshipped, is burned with fire, and all our pleasant things are laid waste." Some of those who did much towards defraying the expense of building that house of the Lord, including several persons of the Bronson family and of the Murray family, have passed onward to their heavenly reward. Soon after the burning of the Gothic church Capt. Abram D. Baldwin opened his large house and kindly invited the people of Greenfield to meet there for the winter to worship the Lord their God.

Though for a time the people were somewhat discouraged and cast down on account of their loss, yet they were not destroyed. Under the leadership of their pastor, Rev. Mr. Sturges, aided by his office bearers, Deacon Wm. B. Morehouse, Deacon John Banks and many others, he said unto the people, "Come, let us arise and build." So they strengthened each other's hands for the good work. As $4,000 insurance money was obtained on the burnt building, and $2,500 had been subscribed by members of the church and society, they engaged with new energy and zeal in the work of building the house of the Lord. In the following month of March, 1854, the society voted to build a new church; and none but those who engaged heartily in the work of building this sanctuary, where we are now assembled, can tell what an amount of labor, time and treasure it cost. But those who did the work and contributed the money know what it cost them. May this house long remain as a lasting monument to their memory.

In this connection, I cannot forbear an allusion to the building of the parsonage at the commencement of my ministry among you, and near the completion of the 150th year of your existence as a church and ecclesiastical society. May the house in which your pastor and his family live, long continue as a token of the generosity of those parishioners who built it. May the builder, Mr. Uriah Perry, and the building committee, consisting of Mr. Morris Murwin, Mr. Oliver Burr, Deacon N. B. Hill, Deacon Wm. B. Morehouse, and all the donors and helpers in the good enterprise of the building the parsonage, experience the truth of the divine promise that "it is more blessed to give than to receive."

We come now to notice the history of the organization of the Greenfield Congregational Church, and to allude to those who have been pastors and ministers of this church.

The following is the original church covenant, subscribed by the Christian professors of Fairfield North-West Parish, *alias* Greenfield, this day, May 18th, 1726, 150 years ago to-day, embodied in a church state by divine allowance:

"We, underwritten, through the strength of Christ, without whom we can do nothing, and in the presence of God and this assembly, do covenant and promise to deny ungodliness and worldly lust, and live soberly, righteously and godly in this present evil world; solemnly avouching the Lord Jehovah to be our God, and the God of our seed, giving up ourselves and ours to be his people, to live to the glory of his great name; solemnly avouching also the Lord Jesus Christ, the only mediator between God and man, to be our Prophet and Teacher, our only Priest and Propitiation, our Supreme Lord and Law Giver, professing ourselves heartily engaged to a sole dependence on His doctrine, to an entire reliance on His righteousness, to a willing obedience to His government; solemnly avouching also the Holy Ghost for our Sanctifier and Comforter, to be led by His conduct, to cherish and entertain His holy motions and influences, subjecting ourselves to the government of Christ in His church, and solemnly engaging to walk one with another in brotherly love, watchfulness and communion, and hereto may Christ Jesus our Lord help us. Amen."

To this covenant subscribed eleven men, namely, John Goodsell, Cornelius Hull, Obadiah Gilburd, John Hide, George Hull, Peter Burr, Daniel Bradley, Theophilus Hull, Jehu Burr, Stephen

Burr, Ebenezer Hull. June 19th, 1726, fifteen women were recommended by some of the neighboring churches, most of them from Fairfield church, and added to this church by the consent of the eleven brethren. On the same day at the organization of the church, Wednesday, May 18th, 1726, Rev. John Goodsell, who had been preaching to the people for some months, was ordained as pastor. Mr. Goodsell was born in Stratford, 1706, graduated at Yale College, 1724. He came here, and was ordained at the age of twenty years. He married Miss Mary Lewis, of Stratford, and they had fifteen children, including a pair of twins, seven sons and eight daughters. Some of the numerous descendants of the Rev. Mr. Goodsell are with us to-day to rejoice in the honorable name which they have inherited from the first pastor of Greenfield church. During the last years of his pastorate he suffered from sickness and infirmity, but departed this life December 26th, 1763, in the 57th year of his age, and his sepulchre is with us unto this day. To show the change in the past 150 years, the following fact is related: Rev. Mr. Goodsell, being the owner of a smart horse, and being in want of a pair of gloves, rode horseback to New York city, bought his gloves and came back the same day. There are not many ministers who can do that now. Under his ministry the church prospered and increased in numbers, so that at the close of the first year of his pastorate it numbered 70 members, 31 of whom were added on the profession of their faith. During his long ministry here of thirty years, the longest of any pastor, 212 persons united with the church by profession, and 256 were received on the half way covenant, as it was called. Of those persons who were baptized and admitted to the church, nine of them were negroes and slaves.

The farmers in the last century owned slaves in Greenfield. Hezekiah Bradley, Esq., a large farmer who lived in the house now occupied by Mr. Millbank, had more than twenty slaves. One of these, called Nance, was kept in the family for three or four generations, and died in the family of James C. Loomis, Esq., of Bridgeport. At length slavery was abolished by law in Connecticut in 1854, and the churches were delivered from its curse and its stain. In August, 1757, the Society voted to send for Rev. Mr. Burritt, of New Fairfield, to come here and preach as a probationer. The following year, May 30th, 1757, put to vote "Whether the Society is willing that Mr. Jonathan Elmer shall be recommended to the association for their advice; whether they think proper to recommend Rev. Mr. Elmer to the Society to preach the Gospel among us, as a probationer." It was voted in the affirmative by a majority of 71 to 9. We suppose the association did not approve of their sending for him, for at a subsequent meeting of the Society, September 2d, 1757, it was put to vote " Whether the Society is willing and desirous to have Mr. Pomeroy to preach with us as a probationer, in order to his settlement in the ministry, and it was voted unanimously in the affirmative by 77 persons."

The committee of the Society, consisting of John Gilbert, Joseph Bradley and Daniel Sherwood, extended the call to Mr. Pomeroy, and he gave an affirmative answer, and December 8th, 1757, was ordained pastor. The committee of arrangements for his ordination were Capt. Moses Diamond, Capt. Daniel Bradley, John Gilbert, Joseph Bradley, Jr., and Daniel Sherwood. The services of the ordination were : Introductory prayer by Rev. Samuel Sherwood, sermon by Rev. Noah Wells, ordaining prayer by Rev. Moses Dickinson, charge to the pastor by Rev. Noah Hobart, right hand of fellowship by Rev. Daniel Buckingham, concluding prayer by Rev. Jonathan Ingalls.

Mr. Pomeroy was born in Northampton, December 14th, 1732, graduated at Yale College 1753, and remained one year after graduation in New Haven, as a Berkeley scholar, a favor granted on account of his superior scholarship. Was tutor in Yale College during the years 1756 and '57. His wife was the daughter of Jonathan Law, Governor of Connecticut, and they had one son who was a clergyman, Rev. Jonathan Law Pomeroy, for some years pastor of the Congregational Church at Worthington, Mass.

Rev. Mr. Pomeroy, second pastor of Greenfield Church for twelve years, was a learned divine, a judicious and excellent pastor, who preached the Gospel faithfully to the people, and died 1770, in the midst of his usefulness, at the early age of 37 years, and His body lies buried in Greenfield Cemetery, with those of his parish, to whom he administered the consolation of the Gospel more than 100 years ago. During his ministry two valuable silver tankards were given to the church for the communion service, one by Deacon Thomas Hill, and inscribed " The gift of Thomas Hill, Esq., to the Church of Christ in

Greenfield, A. D. 1764." The other by Deacon Samuel Bradley, and inscribed "The gift of Samuel Bradley to the Church of Christ in Greenfield, A. D. 1768." These vessels have been used at every administration of the Lord's Sacrament to this church for more than 100 years. During Mr. Pomeroy's ministry, December 13th, 1762, a colony went from Greenfield Church and organized the church in Weston, now Easton. The Easton Congregational Church may be call our eldest daughter, being 113 years old; well may we rejoice therefore in her prosperity. After the death of Mr. Pomeroy, May 20th, 1772, Rev. Wm. Mackey Tennent was invited to become the pastor of Greenfield Church by the large majority of 83 votes. He accepted the call of the Church and Society. He was the son of Rev. Charles Tennent, of White Clay Creek, Delaware, who was younger brother of the more famous preachers, Revs. Wm. and Gilbert Tennent. Mr. Tennent was ordained pastor of Greenfield Church, June 17th, 1772; Deacon Hill, John Bradley and Samuel Bradley, Esqs., were chosen a committee to provide for the ordination. The services of the ordination were: Introductory prayer by Rev. Samuel Camp, sermon by Rev. Samuel Sherwood, ordaining prayer by Rev. Noah Hobart, charge to pastor by Rev. Moses Dickinson, right hand of fellowship by Rev. Noah Wells, concluding prayer by Rev. Jonathan Ingalls.

He graduated at the college of New Jersey, 1763, received the degree of Doctor of Divinity in 1773 from Yale College, and was moderator of the General Assembly in 1777. His wife was the daughter of the Rev. Dr. John Rogers, of New York city. He was a most worthy minister of the New Testament, and an excellent pastor. During his ministry here he had the confidence of his people in a remarkable degree, and kept them together during the war of the American Revolution, when many churches in the United States were scattered and left without a pastor in a low spiritual condition. Mr. Tennent was a man of great sweetness of temper and politeness of manner, and distinguished for hospitality. The society of Greenfield showed their appreciation of his labor, in increasing his salary from time to time, and in giving him annually forty loads of wood. In this record we have proof of their generosity: "*Whereas* the war has greatly enhanced the price of all the necessaries of life to that degree that it is impracticable for Mr.

Tennent, our pastor, to support himself and family on the nominal sum we covenanted and agreed to pay him for his yearly salary; *and, whereas,* in our opinions the enlarging of Mr. Tennent's salary by a public vote might not only have a tendency to depreciate the currency, but also be hereafter made a precedent of, when the currency shall come to a standard and provisions to the old price; for the above mentioned reasons we, the subscribers, hereby agree to pay to Daniel Sherwood, Jr., committee man appointed by this parish to get subscriptions for Mr. Tennent, what we have severally subscribed and annexed to our names, by the first day of March next, or the same pay and deliver unto Mr. Tennent by said time over and above the nominal sum we have agreed to pay to Mr. Tennent for his yearly salary, in order the better to support himself and family in the difficult and extraordinary times, as witness our hands in Greenfield, the 17th November, 1778:"

"Daniel Sherwood, 1½ bushels of wheat; Cornelius Hull, 4 bushels of Indian corn; Eliphalet Hull, 4 bushels of corn; John Alvord, 1 pair of women's shoes; John Hull, 20 weight of butter; Jedediah Hull, 2 bushels of corn and one of wheat; Albert Sherwood, 2 bushels of wheat; Joseph Straton, 6 bushels of wheat; John Straton, 1 bushel of wheat; Stephen Straton, 6 lbs. of flax; Seth Sherwood, 2 bushels of wheat; James Redfield, 15 lbs. of pork; Nehemiah Banks, 40 lbs. of pork; Oliver Middlebrooks, 1 bushel of corn; Ebenezer Banks, ½ bushel of Lisbon salt; Joseph Banks, 1 barrel of cider; Eliphalet Banks, 1 barrel of cider."

After leaving Greenfield Mr. Tennent became pastor of a Presbyterian Church in Abington, near Philadelphia, where he died in the beginning of December, 1810, blessed with an assurance of the favor of his God and Saviour.

At a parish meeting, August 28th, 1752, it was voted to give Mr. Abram Baldwin an invitation to preach the coming winter, but he did not accept of it; for in the following month, October 29th, 1782, the Society voted to send to New Haven to give Mr. Dwight an invitation to preach the gospel to this people. He probably supplied the pulpit afterward most of the time, till his ordination as pastor of Greenfield Church, November 5th, 1783, and his ordination sermon was preached by his uncle, the Rev. Dr. Jonathan Edwards, pastor of a church in New Haven. The committee of arrangements for the ordination of Mr. Timothy

Dwight were: Deacon Joseph Hill, Deacon David Williams, Gershom Hubbell, Esq., Hezekiah Bradley, Esq., and Nehemiah Banks.

The services of the ordination were introductory prayer by Rev. Justus Mitchell, sermon by Rev. Jonathan Edwards, D. D.,* ordaining prayer by Rev. Andrew Elliott, charge to the pastor by Rev. Samuel Camp, right hand of fellowship by Rev. Isaac Lewis, concluding prayer by Rev. Jonathan Murdock.

Dr. Dwight was born at Northampton, 1752, graduated at Yale College 1769, at the head of his class in scholarship, and was tutor in the college from 1771 to 1777, and chaplain in the United States army from 1778 to 1783, and a friend of Washington, representative in the legislature of Massachusetts for one or two years; then was talked of as a member of Congress, but he preferred to become a minister of Christ and a preacher of the gospel. The people of Greenfield were loth to part with him after he was chosen President of Yale College, and protested before the consociation, that was called to consider the expediency of dismissing him from his pastorate here, so as to accept the presidency of the college. Still all the efforts of Greenfield people to keep him were in vain, though he was settled for life, for the consociation dismissed him August 11th, 1795, after a successful pastorate of twelve years.† It was Dr. Dwight's good fortune to honor every position he occupied, and he was undoubtedly the best and greatest divine New England ever produced.

Judge Roger Minot Sherman, of Fairfield, declared "that no man, except the Father of his country, had ever conferred greater benefit on our nation than President Dwight, the fourth pastor of Greenfield Church."

To show you his power as a preacher over his hearers, we have been told that on one occasion he happened to preach in the first church at Bridgeport on morality and honesty, and that the next day several of those who had heard him returned the axes, hoes, forks and other implements of husbandry which they had stolen, or taken without leave. As I was told this fact the thought came to my mind, O! that Dr. Dwight could arise from his grave and preach to those of our day, in our towns, cities, in the State and National Government, who are disposed to rob the public treasury. After his dismission, the church

* *Note E—*Appendix.　　　　　　† *Note F—*Appendix.

was without a pastor for ten years. At a meeting of the Society, November 25th, 1795, it was voted to hire Rev. Mr. Beainfield to preach with us till the last Sunday in December. In the following month of April, 1796, the Society voted to hire the Rev. Dr. Samuel Blatchford for one year.* He was an Englishman, a good scholar and a sound theologian; an acceptable preacher and pastor, and often eloquent in his address; but at the close of his engagement here for one year he left Greenfield and went to Bridgeport, where he became pastor of the first Congregational Church in 1797, and was the father of seventeen children. In March, 1800, Rev. Mr. Yates preached as a candidate for a settlement, and received a call, which he declined to accept. Also the same year, Rev. Mr. Ten Yeck received and declined a call to settle here. In the following year, February 12th, 1801, the Society gave Rev. Stanley Griswold a call to settle with a salary of $560, but he declined the offer. The call to him was renewed June 30th, 1803, and he consented to preach for about a year, when he baptized fifty persons, eight adults and forty-two children. He was a Jeffersonian Democrat, and very popular with a portion of the people, and disposed to administer religious ordinances in a broad church way. In after years he left the ministry, removed to Ohio, was there chosen Senator of the United States, and became Judge of the Supreme Court of that State. On the 10th of November, 1801, a call was given to Rev. Mr. Niles to settle in Greenfield, which he declined. Also, June 7th, 1802, an invitation was extended to Rev. Washington McKnight to settle in the work of the gospel ministry in said Society on a salary of $560. He accepted the call, and the day was appointed for the consociation to meet and effect the union, but objections being presented by a minority of the church before the consociation, he withdrew his acceptance of the call, and the church continued to remain without a pastor. But the majority were so exasperated at losing Mr. McKnight, whom they admired, that they voted, September 9th, 1802, "that Mr. Ward should not preach in the meeting house, although he will preach for nothing." At length the Lord sent to them Mr. Horace Holly, and he was ordained pastor of Greenfield Church September 13th, 1805. The committee of arrangements for the ordination were Gershom Wakeman, Abel Banks, Moses Betts and Thomas Wheeler.

*Note G—Appendix.

The services at the ordination were: introductory prayer by Rev. Platt Buffett; sermon by Rev. Isaac Lewis, D.D.; ordaining prayer by Rev. Matthias Burnett, D.D.; charge to the pastor by Rev. Andrew Elliott; right hand of fellowship by Rev. John Noyes; address to the people by Rev. Justus Mitchell; concluding prayer by Rev. Samuel Goodrich.

Mr. Holly was born in Salisbury, Conn., February 13th, 1781, graduated at Yale College in 1803, ordained pastor Sept., 1805, and dismissed in September, 1808, after a successful pastorate here of three years. He was a distinguished preacher, an eloquent orator, and the Church and Society increased in numbers and prospered under his administration. During his pastorate there were added to the church forty-nine members on profession of their faith, making an average of sixteen each year. While here he was an evangelical minister of the gospel, but there was a change in his theological views when he became pastor of the Holly Street Unitarian Church, Boston, in 1809. After leaving there, he was chosen President of the Transylvania University, Lexington, Kentucky, which office he held nine years. Leaving there, he died on his voyage to New York, of the yellow fever, July 31st, 1827.

Soon after the dismission of the Rev. Dr. Holly, October 11th, 1808, the Society voted to refer a petition to the Legislature of this State, to grant them a lottery for the purpose of raising a fund to assist them in supporting the gospel ministry, and appointed Ebenezer Banks their agent for the above purpose, with full power to employ counsel. For the honor of Christianity, I believe the petition was not granted.

In May 17th, 1810, the Society "voted to give Rev. David Austin a call to take the oversight of the church, so long as he will accept of a three cent tax for his yearly salary, and so long as the Society shall agree to raise a three cent tax for the purpose."

As he would not accept of the offer, the Society "voted at a subsequent meeting, June 28, 1810, to give Rev. David Austin $500 a year instead of the three cent tax voted at the other meeting, so long as he shall continue in discharge of the gospel ministry with us," which was about two years. He was one of the most popular and eccentric preachers of his day, but his reason is supposed to have been affected by an illness of the scarlet fever while pastor of the Presbyterian church, Elizabethtown, N. J. He believed in the literal return of the Israelites to the Holy Land, and that the Jews of the United States would assemble at New Haven, where he built houses for them and a wharf for their use, and from there, the place of Mr. Austin's birth, he believed the Jews would embark for the land of Israel. But with all his errors and eccentricity, he was liked as a preacher on account of his eloquence, intelligence and amiableness of character, and is still remembered with interest by those who knew him. Near the close of his life he became more rational and scriptural in his views, and died in peace, rejoicing in hope of the glory of God.

The society gave a call to Rev. Wm. Belden, Aug. 3, 1812, to settle in the work of the gospel ministry with a salary of $500, which he accepted. Gov. Gideon Tomlinson, David Hull, Esq., and Hull Bradley, Esq., were appointed a committee on the part of the Society to arrange for the ordination of Mr. Belden, that took place October 1st, 1812. The services of the ordination were: introductory prayer by Rev. Sylvanus Haight; sermon by Rev. Mr. Waterman; ordaining prayer by Rev. Isaac Lewis, D. D.; charge to the pastor by Rev. Hezekiah Ripley, D. D.; right hand of fellowship by Rev. Herman Humphrey, D. D.; address to the people by Rev. Daniel Smith; concluding prayer by Rev. John Noyes. He excelled more as a teacher of the youth than as a preacher of the gospel. In both positions he did what he could for the intellectual and spiritual welfare of his flock, over whom the Holy Ghost had made him an overseer, until he was dismissed from his pastorate, April 3d, 1721. After his dismission the pulpit was supplied for a time by the Rev. Mr. Nicholson, an Englishman.

In November 21st, 1821, a unanimous call was given by the Church and Society to the Rev. Richard Varick Dey to settle and become their pastor. He accepted their invitation and was ordained here the 15th day of January, 1823. The committee of arrangements for his ordination were Abram D. Baldwin, David Hill, Thomas B. Osborn, Hull Bradley and Gershom Wakeman.

The services of the ordination were: introductory prayer by Rev. Nathan Burton; sermon by Rev. Stephen W. Rowan, D. D.; ordaining prayer by Rev. John Noyes; charge to the pastor by Rev. Nathaniel Freeman; right hand of fellowship by Rev. Edward W. Hooker; address to the people by Rev. Daniel Smith; concluding prayer by Rev. Henry Fuller.

Being a handsome young man, of commanding presence and natural eloquence, Mr. Dey became very popular and was much admired as a preacher at home and abroad, so that a multitude flocked to hear him, and the old meeting house was not large enough to accommodate the congregation. But, while very popular, he acquired the evil habit of drinking the social glass with some of his distinguished parishioners, and before he was aware of it he drank to intoxication. Thus, a most distinguished preacher and eloquent orator was ruined by intemperance. This having become public, the consociation was called, and by that body of ministers and delegates he was tried and deposed from the ministry. Then, in view of his downfall, all beholders were led to exclaim, "How art thou fallen, oh, Lucifer, son of the morning." After Mr. Dey's dismission the Rev. Samuel Merwin preached the gospel for some time to this people, and received a call to settle as pastor.

For a year or two Rev. Chas. Nicholl supplied the pulpit and preached the gospel to the few who assembled to hear him. Then, in the good providence of God, Rev. Nathaniel Freeman, having been dismissed from the pastorate in Easton, came here as acting pastor and continued in that relation to this people for nearly nine years. Amid many discouragements, trials and afflictions, he preached faithfully the gospel here, and during the time was called to part with his much beloved wife and seven of his children, whose bodies lie buried on Greenfield Hill. But, amid much tribulation, he made full proof of his ministry and died in triumph of a living faith, June 18th, 1864, at the age of 76 years, and his body lies buried beside those of his beloved wife and children.

In 1840 Rev. Rodney G. Dennis, for some months, preached the gospel to this people. In April, 1842, Rev. Thomas B. Sturges was invited to settle as pastor. The invitation having been accepted, Deacon Wm. B. Moorehouse, Deacon Seth Jennings, Samuel Betts and Abram D. Baldwin were chosen as a committee of arrangements for the ordination. The services of the ordination were introductory prayer by Rev. John W. Alvord; sermon by Rev. Edwin Hall, D. D.; ordaining prayer by Rev. Ezra D. Kenney; charge to the pastor by Rev. Noah Coe; right hand of fellowship by Rev. Lyman H. Atwater, D. D.; address to the people by Rev. Theophilus Smith; concluding prayer by Rev. Chauncey Wilcox.

Accordingly, Rev. Mr. Sturges was ordained pastor of the church, June, 1842, and continued in his pastorate here for twenty-five years, until June, 1867. His early ministry was blest with a general revival, as the fruit of which forty-two persons united with the church on the profession of their faith in 1843. But I need not speak of the labors and success of the beloved, wise and faithful pastor, who, for twenty-five years, went in and out among you, preaching Christ and Him crucified. The seed that he sowed bore much fruit, not only during his ministry but the year following his dismission under the continued labors of Rev. R. P. Hibbard and Rev. J. D. Potter, evangelist, when a spiritual harvest of sixty persons was gathered into the church, so that he that soweth and he that reapeth may rejoice together.

My predecessor in the pastoral office, Rev. R. P. Hibbard, was ordained pastor August 4th, 1868; the society's committee for the ordination was Mr. Walter O. Murwin, Mr. John Burr and Mr. Cyrus Sherwood.

Services of the ordination were : introductory prayer by Rev. D. R. Austin; sermon by Rev. Edward E. Rankin, D. D. ; charge to the pastor by Rev. Frederick Alvord; right hand of fellowship by Rev. Martin Dudley; address to the people by Rev. B. J. Relyea; concluding prayer by Rev. George W. Banks.

He was dismissed April 27th, 1872. His character, labors and usefulness are known to all of you. Your present pastor began his labors here, April, 1873, and was installed pastor July 1st, 1873. The Society's committee for the installation consisted of Mr. John Murwin, Deacon Joseph Donaldson and Mr. Andrew Wakeman.

Services of the installation were: invocation and reading of the scriptures by Rev. Franklin S. Fitch; introductory prayer by Rev. B. J. Relyea; sermon by Rev. James W. Hubbel; ordaining prayer by Rev. Martin Dudley; charge to the pastor by Rev. E. E. Rankin, D. D.; right hand of fellowship by Rev. S. J. M. Merwin ; concluding prayer by Rev. Edwin Johnson.

The years that have been the most fruitful in the ingathering of sheaves into the garner of the Lord were the following: 1726, 31 persons ; 1742, 16; 1806, 28; 1807, 11 ; 1843, 42 ; 1849, 17; 1857, 12; 1868, 60 ; 1875, 14. These were years of revival.

In the records of Greenfield Church I do not find any mention of the election of deacons. But among those who have served the church in this important office are the following, namely: Deacons John Hyde, Samuel Bradley, Daniel Banks, Samuel Wakeman, Moses Diamond, Joseph Bradley, Joseph Hill, David Williams, Burr Gilbert, Daniel Bradley, Hull Bradley, Wakeman Lyon, Seth Jennings, Wm. B. Moorehouse, John Banks, N. B. Hill and Joseph Donaldson. The two last are the officiating deacons.

Some of these men, like Deacon Wakeman Lyon, were accustomed to read a sermon and conduct the public worship of the sanctuary when the Church and Society were without a minister. These deacons have been evangelical men, who have honored their office and held fast to the faith as once delivered to the saints. Never will it be known, till the final revelation, what they have done for the spiritual welfare of this church and people. Though most of them are dead, they speak for the good of Zion and the glory of God.

In respect to the Greenfield Sunday School, I find no records, but the school was first organized near the close of the ministry of Mr. Belden, and was under his superintendence; after him Mrs. Eunice Wakeman, wife of Abel Wakeman, then their son, Abel Wakeman, had much to do in the care and superintendence of the Sunday school. After them Rev. Mr. Dey and his wife had the superintendence of the school.

Among the superintendents since have been Governor Gideon Tomlinson, Rev. John Freeman, Dr. Oliver Bronson, Deacon Seth Jennings, Deacon John Banks, superintendent for seventeen years; Deacon N. B. Hill, for six years; Mr. N. W. Ogden, for five years; Mr. Dwight Banks is superintendent the present year. Under the wise superintendence of such men, the Sabbath School has flourished and been a nursery of piety to the Church.

On this account the members of Christ's spiritual household here, " should nourish and cherish it, even as the Lord the Church."

On November 28th, 1869, a Mission Sunday School was organized in Fairfield Woods, and Deacon Joseph Donaldson was chosen superintendent. For three years the Mission Sunday School was held in a private house. But in the summer of 1872 a chapel, now called Hope Chapel, was built by contributions of the members of Fairfield and Greenfield churches, and dedicated December 19th, 1872—Rev. Dr. Rankin performing the dedication services. The Mission Sunday School commenced with thirteen scholars and five teachers, and has prospered so much under Deacon Donaldson and the associate teachers, that the school had an average membership of fifty persons the last year.

If my limits would allow and time permit, I might speak of some of Greenfield's most distinguished citizens; of Gideon Tomlinson, Esq., who was nine years member of the United States House of Representatives, six years member of the United States Senate, and four years Governor of Connecticut, and all these offices he honored. Also I might speak of Walter Bradley, Esq., who was an influential citizen and United States custom house officer for several years and had his office on Greenfield Hill. I might speak of Judge David Hill, who was educated for the gospel ministry, but chose to be a citizen and a leading and influential man of the parish and town, where he held important offices and exerted a controlling influence. I might speak of Capt. Abram D. Baldwin, who was a graduate of Yale College, high sheriff of Fairfield County, and a most worthy, influential and honorable man. I might speak of Dr. Rufus Blakeman, who was a most useful physician and Judge of Probate Court for many years in Fairfield.

I might speak of Ephraim Nichols as a soldier of the American Revolution, who aided by his patriotism in securing the freedom and independence of the United States, and died in Greenfield at the advanced age of ninety-five years. Also I might speak of his son, the Rev. Samuel Nichols, who graduated at Yale College, and was for many years the successful rector of St. Matthew's Church, Bedford, N. Y., from whence he returned to his native town, where he lives in a happy and ripe old age, being, with one exception, the oldest man in the parish.

The oldest man in Greenfield is Mr. Samuel Wilson (gunsmith as he has been called), being ninety-two years old, and the only person I can find who remembers seeing and hearing Dr. Dwight preach.

If time would allow I could speak of Hon. Abram Baldwin, who was a most distinguished lawyer, and chosen, on account of his great learning and ability, Senator of the United States from Connecticut. The following inscription I find on his tombstone in the graveyard on Greenfield Hill : " Abram Baldwin lies buried at Washington. His memory needs no marble. His country is his monument, her Constitution his greatest work." He helped to form the Constitution of the United States, and died while Senator, on the 4th of March, 1807, aged fifty-two years.

But time will not allow me to enumerate any more of the honorable men of Greenfield. Still I must mention the names of those who have served as clerks of the Society and furnished most of the important facts in this historical discourse; such men as Thomas Hill, Moses Diamond, Jr.; Gershom Banks, Samuel Bradley, Jr.; Hezekiah Bradley, Aaron B. Bradley, Gershom Wakeman, Moses G. Betts, Samuel Betts, T. M. Banks, Wm. Bradley and Joseph Betts. I must also mention some of the many men in the learned professions who have been physicians, lawyers, and ministers of the gospel. The following physicians have been citizens of Greenfield: Dr. John Hyde, Eliphalet Hull, David Rogers, Aaron B. Bradley, Daniel Wiggins, Hosea Hulbert, Wm. B. Nash, John B. Paterson, Geo. Dyer, Rufus Blakeman, James B. Kissam and Martin V. Dunham. The following were natives of Greenfield, who became physicians and practised in various places : Doctors Thomas Bradley, Wm. Wheeler, Ebenezer B. Belden, Nathan Bulkley, John Nichols, David Nash, Nathaniel H. Freeman, Geo. B. Banks, Moses Wakeman, Ransom Lyon, Wm. R. Blakeman, Nathan Wheeler and George Nichols.

Of the lawyers who have been citizens or natives of Greenfield we might mention Hon. John Banks, Jehu Burr, Gideon Tomlinson, Abram Baldwin, Thos. B. Wakeman, Daniel Wakeman, Burr Wakeman, Thomas B. Osborn, Thomas Robinson, Geo. B. Kissam, Geo. B. Murray, Effingham H. Nichols, John H. Bradley, Abram Wakeman, Edward B. Sturges and Frank C. Sturges.

Of those who have been natives of Greenfield and clergymen we can name Revs. Aaron Burr, D. D.; Jonathan Law Pomeroy, Sereno Edwards Dwight, D. D., President of Hamilton College; Wm. Theodore Dwight, D. D.; Daniel Banks, Samuel Nichols, David F. Banks, Geo. W. Nichols, Geo. W. Banks and Marcus Burr.

Most of these men in the learned professions of medicine, law and divinity, were graduates of colleges, and a large number of Yale College, who have honored that institution of learning, as well as the place that gave them birth.

We have now given you a brief historical compendium of events pertaining to the Church and Society for the past 150 years, but have not time to allude to the churches of our own and other denominations that have been organized within the limits of the original town of Fairfield. The Fairfield Church' was organized in 1650; Green's Farms Church, 1715; Trinity Church, Fairfield, 1725; Baptist Church, Strafield, 1757; Northfield Church, Weston, 1757; Easton Cong. Church, 1763; Westport Cong. Church, 1832; Southport Cong. Church, 1843; Black Rock Church, 1849; Methodist Church, Flat Rock, Easton, 1789; the West street Methodist Church, Easton, December 12th, 1843; Methodist Church, Westport, 1851; Methodist Church, Southport, 1810.

But, leaving these, I must close with some brief reflections.

From the history of Greenfield Church and Society we should learn how much we are indebted to a virtuous and God-fearing ancestry. They were of the good old Puritan stock, and planted deep in the soil of New England our intellectual, social and religious institutions. Our Church privileges, our schools of learning, our good government, our material advancement, our growth in arts and sciences as well as our happy homes, are the inheritance received from our ancestors.

In view of what they did for us and our children, we should keep them in everlasting remembrance.

I have felt this as I have conversed with the few intelligent and aged fathers and mothers who have told me of what your noble ancestors did in their day and generation. Surely we ought to venerate the names and the characters of those who have done great things for us whereof we are glad, and for whom we should praise the Lord.

Again, from the history of Greenfield Church we learn of God's preserving care and of his faithfulness to his people. Though in the past 150 years this church has passed through great changes, trials and tribulations, yet Zion lives here, because she is engraved upon the palm of God's hand, and her walls are ever before him.

When the prophets, the office bearers, the fathers and mothers in Israel have put off their mortal armor and gone home to their reward, the Great Head of the Church has raised up others to fill their places, and to labor and pray for the spiritual welfare of Zion and for the salvation of the people. In the existence, growth and present prosperity of the church do we not behold God's faithfulness, and his preserving care to his covenanted children from the beginning until now?

Finally, should we not, as members of this church of Christ, be aroused, in view of the inheritance we have received from our fathers, to do with our might the work to which we are called? Should not the past generation who have dwelt on these hill and in these vales, who have done so much for their country and church, arouse us to heroic and godlike action for the good of man and the glory of God? Surely the past generation of your noble ancestors, your own fathers and mothers, grandfathers and grandmothers, do rise up to-day and address you in an audible language and call upon you in the name of your Lord and Master, and urge you, from a regard to them, and to your temporal and eternal welfare, to live for God and for the highest good of the State, the nation and the world.

Do this, friends and parishioners, and act nobly and worthy of the State, the town and the nation that is your birthright; then some future historian, who shall write the historical discourse for the two hundredth anniversary, fifty years hence, will have something to tell of your toils, sacrifices and triumphs in behalf of this church and for the temporal welfare of this society. Nay, more, beloved; do your duty, your whole duty to God, to the church, to society and to your State and country; then future generations will rise up and call you blessed.

In fine, live for God and for the good of humanity; then you will individually accomplish the chief end of man and pass safely through the final ordeal, so that the golden gate of the celestial city will swing wide open as you enter triumphantly, to be greeted by those who have gone before to the promised land. Thus, through a Redeemer's grace "An entrance shall be ministered unto you abundantly into the everlasting kingdom of our Lord and Saviour, Jesus Christ." So may it be, beloved friends, through the grace of our Divine Immanuel, who is " the same yesterday, to-day and forever."

APPENDICES.

Appendix A.

The facts in this discourse I have chiefly obtained from the Connecticut Archives, from the records of Greenfield Ecclesiastical Society, from the historical discourses of Rev. B. J. Relyea and Rev. Dr. Rankin, and from Ebenezer B. Adams, Esq., and others.

Appendix B.

The following persons were summoned May 24th, 1776:

Lieut. Ebenezer Banks, Jr.,
Gershom Banks, Jr.,
Samuel Smith,
Daniel Gershom,
John Sherwood, Jr.,
Elisha Alvord,
John Murwin, Jr.,
John Perry,
Moses Hill,
Mordecai Murwin,
Eliphalet Banks,
David Banks, Jr.,
Ephraim Nichols, Jr.,
Josiah Beardsley.

May 26th, 1776.

Lieut. Lewis Goodsell,
Constable David Down,
Joseph Banks,
Benjamin Smith, Jr.,
John Hubbel, Jr.,
John Down,
Nethemiah Gray,
Burr Jennings,
Jesse Gould,
Nathan Gould, Jr.,
Jesse Burr,
Nehemiah Banks, Jr.,
Ezekiel Oysterbanks.

And so men were summoned, from night to night, as the record shows.

Appendix C.

Thomas Hill,
John Bartram,
David Williams,
Benjamin Gibbard,
. John Burr,
Stephen Burr,
Benjamin Franklin,
Joseph Darling,
John Bradley,
Joseph Barlow,
Joseph Bradley,
Samuel Wackman,
Joseph Wheler,
Ebenezer Lion,
Ignatius Nickeuls,
William Hill,

Obadiah Gilburd,
Joseph Rowland,
Francis Bradley,
George Hall,
Samuel Lyou,
John Lion,
Samuel Lion,
Moses Dimon,
John Gibbard,
Samuel Whitlock,
Samuel Bradley,
Jacob Gray,
Samuel Thorp,
John Smith,
John Smith,
John Smith,
Benjamin Lion,
Samuel Davis,
Thomas Harvey,
Joseph Osband,
Benjamin Darling,
Thomas Turney,
Daniel Adams,
Elijah Crain,
Ebenezer Hull,
Abraham Adams,
Daniel Burr,

Joseph Burr,
Peter Burr,
Daniel Burr,
Misemus Gold,
Josiah Gilbert,
Benjamin Sherwood,
Benjamin Sherwood,
Joseph Sherwood,
Joseph Ogden,
Nathaniel Hull,
William Mallory,
Daniel Williams,
Daniel Bulkly,
Benjamin Banks,
Daniel Bradley,
Peter Sturges,
Peter Smith,
Israel Roulau,
Theophilus Hull,
Moses Ward,
John Green,
John Thorp,
John Hull,
Cornelius Hull,
Joseph Banks,
Jonathan Malory,
John Hide.

Appendix D.

	£	s.
Gershom Banks had pew No. 1 for	14	15
Samuel Bradley, No. 2	16	10
Obediah Hull, No. 3	20	7
Daniel Sherwood, No. 4	12	2
Joseph Hill, No. 5	20	7
Cornelius Hull, No. 6	17	3
Daniel Sturges, No. 7	10	0
Moses Wakeman, No. 8	15	0
David Bradley, No. 9	24	0
Gershom Hubbel, No. 10	26	12
Gershom Bulkley, No. 11	23	15
Jonathan Diamond, No. 12	23	1
John Jennings (2), No. 13	20	7
Gershom Bradley, No. 14	20	3
Reserved for Society, No. 15	—	—
Nehemiah Banks, No. 16	24	0
Ebenezer Banks, No. 17	20	10
Joseph Bradley, Jr., No. 18	27	0

	£	s.
John Banks, No. 19	17	0
Samuel Whitney, No. 20	15	4
David Williams, No. 21	15	0
Benjamin Sherwood, No. 22	17	14
Hezekiah Bradley, No. 23	12	11
Samuel Bradley, Jr., No. 24	23	1
David Banks, No. 25	20	5
Daniel Bradley, No. 26	12	5

Appendix E.

Hear what Rev. Dr. Edwards says in praise of your fore-fathers. "Men, brethren and fathers, we congratulate you on the events of this day. You are now to have a minister set over you in the order of the gospel. We congratulate you on your general and firm union in this affair; on your apparent just sense of the worth and importance of the stated ministration of the divine word and ordinances among you; on your readiness to support the ministry, and your willingness to spend of your worldly substance for this end. By your former punctuality in fulfilling your ministerial contracts, it appears you are not only forward to say but also to do. It is common for the preacher on such occasions as the present to press the duty of support-ing the ministry; but your liberal engagements in the present instance, and your former punctuality in fulfilling your minis-terial engagements, forbid me to say a word on that head. Only pursue the same line of conduct which you have hitherto pursued, and you will acquire honor to yourselves, will be ex-amples to others, and will put it out of the power of your minis-ter to plead necessity for applying himself to secular business, in the neglect of his ministerial work."

Appendix F.

"The Committee presented the votes of the Society, signify-ing their unwillingness that the pastoral relation between Dr. Dwight and them should be dissolved. But Consociation hav-ing taken into serious consideration the importance of the call of Dr. Dwight to the presidency of Yale College, and maturely weighed the circumstances, are of the opinion that his election is a sufficient reason for him to desire a separation from his people, and that it is their duty to consent to it. And having made this declaration, we now think it proper that Dr. Dwight should declare what are his views of duty in the case. Dr. Dwight appeared and declared that he conceived it to be his duty to accept of his appointment. Whereupon (the Committee of the Society declining to make any further opposition to Dr.

Dwight's dismission and withdrawing) the Council proceeded to the following vote : ' That Dr. Dwight be dismissed from his pastoral charge of the Church and Society of Greenfield, and he is hereby accordingly dismissed. When the Consociation reflect upon the great harmony and union which has ever subsisted between Dr. Dwight and the Church and Society of Greenfield, from his first settlement among them as their minister, it is with great pain that they have dissolved a relation cemented by so many years of love and usefulness. But viewing the office of President of an University as one of the most important to the interests of society and religion, principles of benevolence which dictate that a less good should give way to a greater, constrained the Consociation to think it the duty of Dr. Dwight and his people, however dear to each other, to consent to a separation ; wishing them both grace, mercy and peace from God the Father and the Lord Jesus Christ. It is the sincere prayer of the Consociation that the Church and Society of Greenfield may be kept in the same union that hath hitherto prevailed among them, and soon resettle again in the order of the gospel an able and acceptable minister ; and that Dr. Dwight may be made an extensive blessing to society, in training up youth for Church and State.

" ' The above and foregoing voted as the doings of this Council.

" ' Test, JOHN NOYES, Scribe.

" ' GREENFIELD, <i>August 11th,</i> 1795.' "

Appendix G.

Invitation given to Rev. Samuel Blatchford, D. D. " At a parish meeting April 1st, 1796, voted to hire Mr. Blatchford for one year. Voted to give him one hundred and sixty pounds for his services the said year. Voted Walter Bradley, Esq., Daniel Rogers, Elisha and Samuel Bradley, Esq., to make the proposals to Mr. Blatchford. Voted to give $20 to defray the charge of moving Mr. Blatchford to Greenfield.

HEZEKIAH BRADLEY,
Parish Clerk."

A DISCOURSE

IN COMMEMORATION OF

REV. TIMOTHY DWIGHT, D. D., LL. D.,

Fourth Pastor of the Church at Greenfield Hill, and afterwards President of Yale College.

BY TIMOTHY DWIGHT,

PROFESSOR IN YALE THEOLOGICAL SEMINARY.

On the 19th of May, 1783, the people of this parish, by a unanimous vote, extended an invitation to a young man residing in Northampton, Mass., to become their pastor. According to the custom of the period, he had preached here for a number of Sabbaths, and had spent so much time with the people as to give them sufficient knowledge of his character and gifts. They had, doubtless, heard favorably of him, also, from the college where he had been employed as a tutor for six years, and where he had gained many friends and a high reputation. They looked forward, in all probability, in case of his acceptance of their call, to a long-continued ministry on his part among them, and to his living and dying in their community. We can realize something of the hopes and fears with which they awaited his decision, for, in these days as well as those, the people of a parish are always thus deeply interested when they are brought to a hearty unanimity in the choice of a minister. He gave them his answer, which was a favorable one, on the 20th of July following. The letter containing his reply is found in the records of the church, and is in these words: "I have considered the unanimous invitation given me by the church and congregation of Greenfield to settle with them in the gospel ministry, and the proposal they have made me for my support in that office. In answer to this invitation, I beg leave to observe that the unanimity and friendliness of the call are so agreeable, and the proposals so handsome, that I esteem it my duty to accept of them, and do hereby give my cheerful consent to settle with this church and people on the plan and according to the principles I have uniformly delivered to you, particularly in two sermons, the one from Acts, xx. 26th and 27th, and the other from the first to the Corinthians, vii. 14th,* and I desire your constant prayers to Almighty God that I may be a blessing to you." On the 5th of November in the same year he was ordained, the Consociation of the neighboring churches taking part in the work, and giving him the right hand of fellowship. The circumstances leading to the establishment of this pastoral relation, and the solemn service which inaugurated it, were similar to those which had often occurred before that time, and have been often repeated since in the towns of New England. But the minister, who on this day began here the real work of his life, was destined to be one of the leading men of his age, and to be remembered in after times for his power and influence. And for this reason it is that on this occasion, when we are met to celebrate the completion of a century and a half of the history of this church, it has been regarded as fitting that this one of the long line of its pastors should be specially commemorated.

The young man of whom I have spoken was Timothy Dwight. Born in the year 1752, he was now 31 years of age. He had graduated at Yale College with high honor fourteen years before, in 1769, and after teaching, during the interval, in the grammar school in New Haven, had been appointed tutor in the college in 1771. Here he continued until 1777. On the 3d of March, in this last named year, he was married at the house of Pierrepont Edwards, Esq., of New Haven, to Miss Mary Woolsey, daughter of Benjamin Woolsey, of Dosoris, L. I., and on the 4th of September following he was commissioned as a chaplain in the army of the Revolution. He remained in this office until March, 1779, when, in consequence of the tidings of his father's death in a remote part of the country, he offered his resignation, and returned to his home in Northampton to aid his mother, who had been left with limited means

---

* Acts xx. 26, 27.—"Wherefore I take you to record this day, that I am pure from the blood of all men, for I have not shunned to declare unto you all the counsel of God." 1st Corinthians, vii. 14.—"For the unbelieving husband is sanctified by the wife, and the unbelieving wife is sanctified by the husband: else were your children unclean, but now are they holy."

and with a large family of children, of whom he was the eldest. While residing in Northampton he had almost constantly supplied vacant pulpits in the neighborhood, and both in this way and through his duties as a chaplain, he had already had considerable experience as a preacher. He had, indeed, been invited to take the pastoral office in Charlestown and in Beverly, Mass., and, in connection with the latter of the two invitations, it is said that he was promised a professorship in Harvard College. But, in consequence of the importance of his presence and assistance at home, he had declined these offers. The call from this parish came at a time when he could more easily be spared, and accordingly, having decided to accept it, he came here with his family, consisting at that time of his wife and two young children, to enter upon his first, and, as it afterwards proved, his only pastorate.

The date of his installation was two months after the final and definitive treaty of peace was signed, by which the independence of the United States was acknowledged by Great Britain, and two years after the last great battle of the Revolutionary war. Only four years before, the adjoining villages of Fairfield and Green's Farms had been burned by the British troops, and even now they had scarcely recovered their old state after this devastation. This parish had a population of 1,000 or 1,100 souls, scattered over a tract of country of about fifteen square miles in extent, with a small central village of some fifteen houses in the immediate neighborhood of the church. It was, as he describes it himself, one of the smallest parishes in Connecticut in territorial extent, but, considering this fact, one of the most populous. The people were almost exclusively farmers. Possessed of an excellent soil and in the midst of delightful scenery, they passed their lives in the simple, yet honorable way which characterized our New England fathers. We can easily picture to ourselves the intelligent and godly people as they assembled on that November day in their plain meeting house, which many of the older persons in this audience will remember, to welcome their new pastor to his new office.

The sermon delivered on the occasion was by the Rev. Dr. Jonathan Edwards, of the Whitehaven Church in New Haven, an uncle of the pastor elect, and the second son of the celebrated President Edwards. Its subject was, "The Manifestation of the Truth the End of Preaching." It was based upon the text found in Second Corinthians, iv. 2*. Few in this audience, probably, would be interested in a perusal of this sermon, but in the portion of it which contains the more special address to the pastor, occurs a passage which shows the character both of the speaker and of him to whom the words were spoken. In urging upon the new pastor the duty of being faithful in his researches after truth, the preacher said: "Improvement is by no means at an end; and those men err exceedingly who lament that they live in this late period of the world, wherein improvement and science have been anticipated, and there is no room left for further discoveries. There is abundant room for discovery and improvement in every science, and especially in theology." When we remember that this installation service took place not only before the first steamboat floated on the waters of the Hudson, but before the idea even of propelling vessels by steam had occurred to Fitch or to Fulton; when we remember that it was after the lifetime both of the preacher and of the young pastor had ended, that the first railway was constructed, and within the lifetime of their grandchildren that the electric telegraph was invented; when we remember that the wonderful development of modern science in our land, in all its branches, had its beginning years later than this, we cannot but smile at the thought of those who were bewailing the fact of their living only after all that was to be discovered had already been made known. If those worthy individuals could but return for the day, and come with us who have come from other towns and cities to this place this morning, and if they could go with us as we return to our homes, and see the things which they never dreamed of having become the familiar and essential accompaniments of our daily life, how strange would their old lamentations appear! If those among them who lived on Greenfield Hill could stand here again, and, while they were looking out upon the same beautiful prospect with which they were once familiar, could know the altered mode of life and the thousand peculiar comforts of these modern days, they would, indeed, feel that the old world had entered into a new existence. But these two men—the elder

* 2d Cor. iv. 2. "But having renounced the hidden things of dishonesty; not walking in craftiness nor handling the word of God deceitfully, but by manifestation of the truth, commending ourselves to every man's conscience in the sight of God."

and the younger alike—were not among this number. They believed in the future. They hoped for and prophesied a better and larger and higher life for their children's children than they knew themselves. And even in theology—while they did not doubt that the truth of God was ever the same—they believed that devout and earnest men would be continually making new discoveries, and would be bringing their human statements nearer and nearer to the divine standard.

The people of this parish are to be commended for the provision which they made for the support of the new pastor and his family, for, though the sum may seem small in these days— $500, together with a parish lot of six acres and twenty cords of wood annually (there being a provision of $1,000 for "settlement," as it was called)—the salary is said to have been the largest given in the State at that time. Indeed, more than thirty years afterwards, when writing of the condition of the ministry in this respect, at a time when the price of all the means of subsistence had been doubled, this pastor himself says: "The average salary of ministers in Connecticut, including all the perquisites annexed to it, does not, I believe, exceed four hundred dollars. There are, perhaps, from six to ten within two hundred and fifty dollars. I know of but one which amounts to eleven hundred dollars." Doubtless the salary was made as large as possible, because the reputation of the young man whom they called was already so high, and the prospects for his future were so flattering. But the people, if they had not been of liberal minds and in perfect harmony both with one another and with him, would not have surpassed in their pecuniary offers even the churches of larger and more central towns.

With such unanimity and such provision for his support on the part of the parish, Mr. Dwight began his work here. He had now fully entered on the profession to which he had consecrated his life, and for which he had given up all the attractions of the practice of law and of the political sphere, though these were very great in his case, and though many of his friends, who saw a brilliant career before him if he did so, had urged him strongly to yield to their influence. The life of a village pastor, at all times, is one without much of incident that is interesting to the world at large or to the generations that follow. Useful, and bearing in its work upon the Christian life of

many souls, it is hidden from the public gaze, and when we try
to trace out its history, we find that the memory of its facts has
passed away with the period to which it belonged. For some
reason—probably because of the scantiness of the records which
he made, owing to the permanent weakness of his eyes—the
recorded incidents of this pastor's career in this place are unusually few in number. We know, however, that in the course
of the years which he spent in Greenfield, he conceived the
plan of that system of theology which he afterwards carried out
in his ministry in Yale College, and that he preached the
greater part if not all of these discourses, in their earliest form,
to the people here. They were delivered from brief notes, his
custom being not to speak from a carefully written manuscript,
but only from a few leading thoughts committed to paper, and
with a reliance upon the inspiration of the hour for the language
which he should employ. According to the record of an aged
person connected with this church, who died a few years since,
these sermons or lectures were given on Wednesday evenings;
but if they were, our fathers must have been more ready for
instruction in doctrinal theology, in their weekly meetings, than
their descendants are. In those days, however, theological discussion was very widespread in the community. The New England mind, we may say, became what it was because all men,
high and low, thought both on politics and theology—the two
subjects of deepest interest connected with the problems of this
life and the life to come.

It is stated that Mr. Dwight prepared and preached nearly
one thousand sermons during the period of his settlement here;
but among them these were the ones that in their subsequent
and more perfect form were destined to give him his extended
fame. Few churches certainly, even in the larger cities of the
country, had the opportunity to listen to such eloquent and
powerful presentations of the gospel truths as those which were
heard from the pulpit of this church during the twelve years
of that pastorate. "The people of the neighboring towns," it
is said, "often resorted to Greenfield to hear his discourses; and
an intimation that he was to preach in any particular place
rarely failed to attract a full audience." We know, also, that
as a Christian teacher he built up the church both in graces
and in numbers, keeping them in the happy harmony which
had been so conspicuous as they received him at the first, until

the very latest period of his residence with them, and gathering into the fellowship of believers a goodly company, whose religious life was first awakened by his influence. We know, still further, that he gave a new character and life to the village. By reason of his wide and continually widening acquaintance with literary and distinguished men, and his abounding hospitality, Greenfield became, as one of his sons has said, " the resort of learning, of talents, of refinement and of piety." " His doors were ever open," says the same person, " to welcome the stranger as well as the friend;" and he adds, " we believe the instances to be rare in which a single individual has been the centre of such extensive attraction to men of superior character, or so entirely altered the aspect of society around him." It is not strange, then, that the people here were proud of having him among them, and felt honored by the presence of a man whose fame—which, as they saw, must constantly grow greater—would draw the thoughts of many in distant regions to the place where he lived. The charm of his society and conversation, also—the memory of which has come to our own days through the testimony of all who knew him — must have rendered life in this beautiful village a richer and more beautiful thing than it had ever been before. Every man and woman—every child, even—must have delighted in meeting him, for, with an extraordinary faculty of entering into the experience and pursuits of all classes and ages, he had always the kindliest and most instructive word to suit the wants of all. Awake to everything that was true and good, he was beyond all question here, as, indeed, he was everywhere, a power in the community which every one was glad to recognize and quick to feel.

A prominent thing in his history here, and, at the same time, a thing which affected and influenced the parish greatly, was the school which he established soon after the beginning of his pastorate. Ever since the years in which, with very marked success, he had held the tutorship in Yale College, his thoughts and interests had centered largely in the work of teaching. In Northampton, after retiring from the army, he had carried on a day school in addition to his other occupations, in which he was assisted by Joel Barlow, who was afterwards the distinguished politician, and who was already gaining some reputation as a poet. We may suppose, therefore, that it was in consequence

of his love for the work of teaching, as well as in order to increase his means of support, that he early established here
the school which soon became so celebrated throughout the
country. It is stated that more than a thousand pupils were
educated in this school. They came from all parts of the land,
and some of them, in later years, attained high stations in civil
life. Among these were Henry Baldwin, who was one of the
Justices of the Supreme Court of the United States, and Joel
R. Poinsett of South Carolina, who became Secretary of War
during the administration of President Van Buren. It is to be
regretted that no complete list of these pupils has been preserved, but enough is known to make it manifest that a quickening life was infused into the village by the existence of the
school and the ingathering here of so many intelligent young
people. Nor should we fail to state that the school was de-
signed for both sexes, and that, at one time at least, it was declared—no doubt with great confidence that no one in any other
place would venture to contradict the statement or maintain
the opposite—that Dr. Dwight's class of young ladies included
the most beautiful ever assembled in a class together. Among
these were three daughters of Mrs. Burr, of Fairfield, worthy
daughters of a mother whom Dr. Dwight himself describes as
"adorned with all the qualities which give distinction to her
sex, and as possessing fine accomplishments and a dignity of
character scarcely rivalled." When we think of these young
men and maidens rambling and playing in company, and talk-
ing together of the joyous and hopeful things of life, we cannot
be surprised that the record of the aged member of this church,
to which I have already referred, should say, in view of it all,
"Those were lively times in Greenfield." He was, perchance,
recalling in his extreme old age, with something of fond regret,
the delightful memories of the far distant days of his own
youth, and thinking, as we all do, when the years are bearing
us onward towards the end, of the brave hearts and beautiful
souls that we once knew and loved, while they and we were
alike full of our early enthusiasm. Certain it is that the
presence of such a company, representing the best families in
the land, and sent hither for instruction and discipline preparatory to their future life, must have changed the character of
the place in no ordinary degree. From a quiet parish, with the
stillness of the farmer's work, it became full of merry voices and

healthful with the influences of higher education. The school was not limited in its aim and plan to the studies introductory to the collegiate course, but young men came even from the classes in Yale College, and placed themselves voluntarily under the charge of so eminent a teacher.

It is especially noticeable that Dr. Dwight enlarged the sphere of instruction for his female pupils, introducing them to the knowledge of higher branches in literature and learning than had been opened to them in the earlier history of the country. He believed in the nobleness of women, not only as moral but as intellectual beings. He devoted himself to their higher cultivation with as much ardor and energy as he ever gave to that of young men. It is not the least of the glories of his life that he was a leader in this work, and was in advance of his age in regard to it as truly as he was in any sphere of his efforts. He greatly enjoyed the society of refined and intelligent women, respecting and honoring them for what they were, and, with readiness and gladness, he contributed from the rich stores of his own learning and thought to make their daughters still more intelligent and refined than themselves.

So he labored, and such was the result which he accomplished in this place. But it was not possible that such a man should be limited in his power and influence to his own immediate field of labor. He rapidly became one of the most prominent among the ministers of the State, and was known and respected by the clergy of other States and other denominations. In the year 1787 he was honored with the degree of Doctor of Divinity by the College of New Jersey, at Princeton. This mark of distinction was less common and of greater value at that period than it is in these more recent times. In his case it was bestowed at an unusually early age, for he had only entered upon his thirty-sixth year. The record of his history, however, shows us, in all its parts, that he had not only become more widely known, but had accomplished greater results, before he reached the middle point of human life, than even men of ability and eminence often do. I may add here, in passing, that a number of years afterwards he received the degree of Doctor of Laws from Harvard College, and that thus he was recognized as worthy of special distinction by the two leading institutions of learning in the country, besides the one where he had been educated.

By reason of the prominence which he had gained he was very influential in the religious and ecclesiastical movements of the day. One among these, in which he had a leading part while he was still residing here, was the union of the Presbyterian and Congregational churches according to a plan by which the Western States were left open to the former body alone. Without entering on the discussion of this subject here, and without meaning to assert that he could certainly have foreseen what followed in the succeeding half or three quarters of a century, I may be permitted to say that, in my judgment, his position in this matter was a mistaken one, and that the plan which he favored was a plan by which the grand principles of Congregational freedom were wholly surrendered to a centralized ecclesiastical organization everywhere outside of the narrow limits of New England. The children and grandchildren have been wiser than the fathers were in this regard, and the council of 1852, whose presiding officer, it may be remarked, was his own son, Dr. Wm. T. Dwight, finally placed Congregationalism at the West on the same firm foundation which Presbyterianism had gained so long before.

During his life in Greenfield Dr. Dwight published both of the two longer poems which are known as connected with his name. One of them was written here. The "Conquest of Canaan" had been originally composed before he was twenty-three years of age, having been begun even when he was only nineteen. According to the statement of his son, in his biography, "proposals for printing this poem were issued in 1775, and upwards of 3,000 subscribers procured; but the circumstances of the country, just then commencing the war of Independence, which lasted till 1783, postponed its publication." It was finally printed in 1785. Possibly the date of its appearance before the public has given the impression that this poem was a work of his maturer life, and as such has subjected it to criticism. Dr. Dwight was not a poet of a high order, certainly—perhaps, as some one has said, "he was only almost a poet, but not quite." But we must not forget that he and his contemporaries are not to be judged by the standard of to-day. When we remember that poetry had scarcely seen its earliest beginnings in this country at that time, and that the poems of Percival, who wrote more than forty years afterwards, are clearly not to be measured with the works of our own age; when we remember, also, that everything in that day was so largely under the demoralizing influence of the style of Pope, and that modern freedom and individuality were quite unknown; and when we remember that Dwight and his companions wrote in their early years, I think they may fairly be regarded as worthy of their due measure of praise for what they attempted and achieved. It is almost as idle and unreasonable to pronounce upon them a condemnatory judgment, because they did not reach the standard of to-day, as it would be to criticise the fathers of modern science in this country, who did so great a work for their own time, in comparison with those who are in possession of all the knowledge and discoveries of these recent years. What was the literature in prose in our nation one hundred years ago, and how long is it since our English cousins were first compelled to acknowledge that a book in general literature, worthy of their reading, had been written in America?

The other principal poem, to which reference has been made, is entitled "Greenfield Hill." It was written mainly in 1787, and, as its author says, "was begun with no design of publishing it, but with the aim merely to amuse his own mind and to gain a temporary relief from the pressure of melancholy." Hence it was composed only at intervals, and was laid aside "when other avocations or amusements presented themselves." As its name would indicate, it is founded upon the scenery and life of the village where he lived, but it is not so closely connected with it as to become in any complete measure descriptive of either. There is less of stateliness, and more of freedom and variety in the style and metre, than in the *Conquest of Canaan*, and consequently it is more interesting to a reader at the present time. The idea of the poem was, probably, founded upon that of Goldsmith's *Deserted Village*. The original design was to imitate the style of different British poets, though this design was not fully carried into execution. It does not become this occasion, nor indeed does the time permit, that I should attempt to criticise this poem, or set forth its merits or demerits. I would, however, that every minister in our ancient Commonwealth had the ability to charm away his melancholy hours with poetry of his own making, that should be even as sweet, and as truly inspired by the Muses, as that which this book contains. And yet, as one of these ministers, and at the same time a descendant of his own, I have to acknowledge that

—whatever may have been Dr. Dwight's claims in this regard for himself—he had not poetry enough in his constitution to transmit it either in his own family or to the apostolic succession to which he belonged. Though both of his poetical works were republished in England, they, neither of them, ever reached a second edition in that country or in this, and I presume it may possibly be the fact that not a single copy of the poem called Greenfield Hill can now be found in the parish of Green field Hill.

In the midst of these employments, and surrounded by his pupils and his parishioners; occupying his busier hours with earnest labors for the good of others, and his quieter ones with the most refining and elevating mental work; with the tender love of an honored wife, and the happy voices of his children, four of whom were given to him here, filling his home and his heart with delight, he moved on in his unostentatious yet most honorable career for twelve years. The people had come more and more fully, as time advanced, to feel that he had created for himself a sphere from which he could not well be spared, and to believe that he would remain with them always. But, doubtless, in his own mind, he had thought of the day as probably coming when some wider field, limited by the bounds of no single parish, should open to him, and we can scarcely hesitate to believe that he had known something of the public feeling which, for some years, had been turning towards him as the person who should one day fill the highest office in the College at New Haven. Indeed, even as early as 1777, when, at the age of twenty-five, he was just closing his service as tutor in the college, the students, it is said, had drawn up a petition that he might be made President—a petition which would have been presented to the corporation had it not been for his own interference. It was natural, therefore, that, as the administration of President Stiles was seen to be drawing towards its close, by reason of his advancing age, Dr. Dwight should be pointed out as the probable successor, and that he should himself be cognizant, in some degree, of this fact.

When, accordingly, on the 25th of June, 1795, a few weeks after the death of Dr. Stiles, the corporation of the college assembled and elected him to the presidency, it could not have been a great surprise to his own mind. To his parishioners, however, if not altogether a surprise, it was a grievous disappointment of their hopes. It cannot be thought strange that they earnestly opposed his acceptance of the offered office, and that when his own reflection upon the subject led him to call a meeting of the consociation of churches to which he belonged, to advise him respecting his course, they unanimously voted "that the inhabitants of this place are unwilling that he should accept of his appointment to the presidency of Yale College, and take a dismission from the people of his charge." A large committee, consisting of twelve persons, was appointed to represent the Church and Society before the consociation, and to urge their claims as against those of the college. This committee, however, was unsuccessful in its effort, for the consociation, without any dissenting voice, advised the dissolution of the pastoral relation and the removal of Dr. Dwight to the new position. The tradition is, that the people here were so outraged in their feelings by this action, that they would never consent afterwards to hear any minister, who took part in this decision, preach in their pulpit. We smile, perhaps, at this course of the fathers and grandfathers so many years ago; but we look upon the whole matter with the knowledge of the past history, and in the light of to-day, while they saw it only as surrounded by the circumstances then present, and without any possibility of foreseeing what was to come.

New Haven, which has now become a city of sixty thousand inhabitants, had, in 1790, only about four hundred more than Fairfield. The latter place has continued nearly as it then was, and this parish is but little larger, I suppose, than in the year when Dr. Dwight began his ministry here. But how little idea of such a change did the men of that day have, or could they have had! The college, also, in 1795, had but one hundred and ten students. Though it was of importance to the commonwealth, it was a small institution. The consociation, however— as we of this era, who look back upon his life so long after its ending, clearly see—were in the right, and the people of the parish in the wrong. In communicating to the corporation his acceptance of the position which they offered him, Dr. Dwight used the following language: "Allow me, gentlemen, to say, that few undertakings in human life appear to me to be fraught with more difficulties than this one on which I am now venturing. It is a consolation to reflect that, when faithfully pursued, there are not many which are more beneficial to mankind. The

Most High hath been pleased in his providence to call me to this employment. I feel myself obliged, though not without great diffidence, to obey the summons." Who can doubt that it was, indeed, the Divine summons, and that his obeying it, as he did, was the undertaking of a work most beneficial to mankind ?

The population of this parish, at the time of his resignation of the pastorate, probably did not exceed thirteen hundred. The graduates of Yale College, during his administration of twenty-two years, including the three succeeding classes who came, in some measure, under his influence, numbered thirteen hundred and one. But these graduates were all men who were destined, in the future, to take prominent positions in the larger or smaller communities where they should find their homes. Many of them were to have a lasting fame and power among mankind. When we look at such names as Moses Stuart, and Lyman Beecher, and Nathaniel W. Taylor, and Eleazar T. Fitch, and Chauncey A. Goodrich, and Asahel Nettleton, in the field of theology and religious effort; or at those of John C. Calhoun in the sphere of statesmanship, or Samuel F. B. Morse in invention, or Benjamin Silliman in science, or Thomas H. Gallaudet in creating a new life for those to whom speech is denied, or James A. Hillhouse, and John Pierpont, and James G. Percival in poetry, or Alexander H. Stevens and Edward Delafield in medicine, or Theodore Strong and Alexander M. Fisher in mathematics, or Roger S. Baldwin and Samuel J. Hitchcock in the law, or James L. Kingsley and Ethan A. Andrews in classical scholarship, who of us can begin to measure the effect of that influence which a man like Dr. Dwight was able to exert upon the world through the stimulating and elevating power which he imparted to them? Each of these thirteen hundred graduates would become a means of transmitting his teachings and his inspiration to others, and the circle of his life would thus be widened to reach the most distant places, and even the generations of the future. No such power could have been realized in this church, or in any other church in the commonwealth or the country. The people of this parish would, almost all of them, have lived and died on the soil here, by the very necessity of the case; but among those thirteen hundred graduates nearly three hundred became ministers of the gospel, some of whom carried its message to remote and heathen lands; nearly seventy became presidents or professors in colleges or professional schools; and about one hundred held the offices of highest executive, legislative or judicial trust in the States or the nation. And all of these men, to their latest years, bore with them, as we have abundant testimony, the grateful recollection of what he had done for them, and the impress of his mind and character upon their own. However widely they differed among themselves, they were all united in their admiration for their teacher, so that Yale College became to every one of them indissolubly connected with his name. It would, indeed, have been a loss of one of the grandest opportunities for a man, and of one of the grandest men for an opportunity, which the history of the country has ever known, had this eminent teacher remained in the pastoral charge of any church, and declined the invitation which came to him at this critical moment of his life.

On the 8th of September, 1795, Dr. Dwight was formally inducted into the office of president, and on the following day he began his public duties by presiding at the exercises of the college commencement. The college was, at that time, just closing the first century of its existence as an institution. It was about to enter not only on a new period, but also, in the highest and most complete sense, on a new era of its history. The trustees had said, in their letter which communicated to him his election, "The circumstances of this seminary are such as greatly need a president, and require his presence and exertions in office." But even they had, probably, a very inadequate idea of the full significance of their own words. Up to this time it had been a day of small things. The institution, as we may almost say, had been a collegiate school rather than a college. The instruction and government had been in the hands of the president, in connection with a small body of tutors who remained in office but two or three years, and consequently had no permanent influence. Only two professorships had ever been established—that of divinity and that of mathematics and natural philosophy—and, at this time, the latter alone had an incumbent. The funds were exceedingly limited. The number of students, as we have already seen, was comparatively small. The course of instruction included none of the natural sciences except astronomy and physics, and even in these branches and in the ancient languages the means at command for studying them, and the progress made by the students, were, as viewed from the standpoint of later days, insignificant. Professional education in separate departments of a university, as we are now familiar with it, had not been provided for and had scarcely been thought of. And yet the opening era was soon to call for growth and development in all these directions. The man who should be adequate to the emergency must be no ordinary man. He must have the clearness of perception to see farther than those around him, and the earnestness in action which would make him ready for every exigency and every work. In the light of the facts and records of the subsequent years, unless I am wholly unable to read them correctly, it is clear that such a man was found in President Dwight.

The presiding officer of a college, according to that arrangement of things which has been known in almost all institutions of this kind in our country, has an intimate connection with its instruction, its discipline, its pecuniary interests, and all the plans for its improvement and growth. This was, of course, the fact in Yale College at the close of the last century, in a higher degree even than it now is, for then, as we have seen, he stood almost alone, so far as any permanent instructors were concerned, while to-day he is surrounded by more than fifty professors. But no college in any period of its history can make continued and healthful progress, if its president is characterized by inefficiency or by a want both of energy and wisdom.

It will be impossible, on the present occasion, to give a complete history of Dr. Dwight's administration; but no discourse relating to his career would be, in any measure, complete without a reference to some of the things which he accomplished.

In regard to the plans for the enlargement and progress of the institution, he had scarcely assumed his office before he entered earnestly and enthusiastically upon the consideration of them. It is a fact worthy of notice, that he fixed his thoughts upon a young man in the very first senior class which he instructed, as a person who might well be called to teach in the college the science of chemistry, which was then in its infancy in the country—that he urged the corporation to establish a professorship in this department as early as 1798—and that, within six years from his accession to office, he had secured the necessary endowment for the purpose, and was enabled to place the person whom he had chosen in the new position. The large minded comprehensiveness with which, at that early day, he perceived the importance of this branch of learning, and provided for its introduction into the curriculum of study, was only equalled by the sagacity with which he saw, at the age of twenty, the powers and future possibilities of Benjamin Silliman. In the same year that Mr. Silliman was elected to this professorship, measures were instituted for establishing a professorship of the ancient languages, and already in the previous year a professor of law had been appointed. Though this last named officer was expected to instruct only the undergraduates in the general principles of law, there is some reason to believe that the idea of a professional school in this department, as a thing of the future, entered his mind. Within eleven years after he came to New Haven the first steps were taken towards the founding of a medical school, the organization of which was authorized by the Legislature of the State in 1810, and was completed by the appointment of four able professors in 1813. I may add that, when in 1806 the earliest movements were made towards the founding of a theological seminary at Andover, Mass.—the first one established in the country—he was consulted by those most prominently engaged in the enterprise; and, according to one who was acquainted with the facts of the case, he did much for the accomplishment of the end. Dr. N. W. Taylor, the person to whom I refer, says that " he entered into the subject with the deepest interest, unfolding his views of the advantages and necessity of such an institution, and that he seemed to exult as an eye witness of its great and blessed results." His participation and interest in that great work are, also, proved by the fact that, when the seminary was formally opened, he was the person invited to preach the inaugurating discourse. But, to our present purpose it is more important, and at the same time a thing still more worthy of notice, that, when these gentlemen came from Massachusetts to get his advice and counsel respecting the institution there, he told them that he " had long had it in his heart to extend the means of a thorough preparation for the ministry in the college at New Haven," and that " should the time come when this should be done, and the graduates of Yale should be induced to pursue theological study at a seminary connected with the college, it must not be considered as interfering with their undertaking." Indeed, at an early day, he induced his eldest son, who bore his own name, to invest a certain sum of money which should, in the course of a few years, provide for the establishment of a professorship in theology. There can be no doubt, also, that he fixed in his own mind upon Dr. Taylor as the one who should occupy this position, and that thus, in these two essential points, he laid the plan for the beginning of a theological seminary in New Haven. Moreover, he had classes, from time to time, of graduate students, whom he persuaded to remain at the college and prepare themselves for the ministry under his charge—in this way, as it were, starting a school, as centered in himself, before it was possible that it should be formally organized. The theological department of the college was not founded, indeed, until five years after his death, but he was as truly its originator as if he had lived to see and rejoice in its progress.

All this that has been said shows how widely his mind opened itself to consider everything in every department which the coming times would demand, or which could make the college greater or more truly a blessing than it had ever been before. He grasped the idea of a University—a place of universal learning, and a place where the young men of the country should be more perfectly educated for the learned professions, as well as in the general studies which might be preparatory to the life of any cultivated gentleman. Not only did he grasp this idea, but he carefully formed his plans, and stimulated others to interest in them, and put forth most earnest efforts and seized upon every opportunity for their accomplishment, and rested not for a moment till the end was attained. It is remarkable, also, that, with a wonderful insight into the human mind and character, and with an equally wonderful foresight of the future, he selected for the new chairs of instruction which were created, a body of extraordinary young men—graduates of the early years of his own presidency—who should assist him in his great work. They were men, in greater or less degree, of a spirit kindred to his. He inspired them constantly with his own enthusiasm, filled their minds with undoubting confidence in and admiration for himself, opened to them the vision of great things which floated before his imagination, encouraged them in their every undertaking, and was a tower of strength to them in every hour of their disappointment. They all knew that they could go to him and find hearty sympathy: that his wide circle of interest and knowledge included the fields in which they were each of them employed; and that even if, in their own special line, they passed beyond the boundaries of what he knew, his heart was large enough to believe in the value of that which they were reaching after, and generous enough to aid them as if he were wholly within their own sphere of working. What estimate can be placed upon the power and helpfulness of such a man in a great institution of learning in any period of its history? To his colleagues his society and counsel are an incalculable blessing. To the college his influence is an element of the highest life. Surely Dr. Dwight was all that has here been represented, if we may believe the evidence of what he accomplished—and not simply this, but also the unvarying testimony of these younger associates, given long after his death and in their own old age.

The material prosperity of the college was also an object of his special thought. He appreciated the necessity of far larger means, provided the results desired were to be reached. By private solicitation and public effort he sought to secure such means, and on two or three occasions he made powerful appeals to the legislature of the State—a body which has, in almost all cases, whether in his day or in ours, resisted the most eloquent presentations of the cause of our higher institutions of learning. Perchance it has been better for the college that it has received so little from the State. Certainly it is so, if the effect of public gifts would have been to bring it in any measure under legislative control. But, with little or no assistance from the State authorities, the funds of the college were becoming gradually larger, and the buildings of the institution were repaired and increased in number. Within six years after the beginning of Dr. Dwight's presidency the number of students had nearly doubled. In consequence of this great increase a new building for their accommodation was erected, and also another building which afforded new and better recitation rooms, as well as a place for the chemical laboratory and the library. The library itself was also enlarged, and considerable sums were expended for the chemical and philosophical apparatus. As an illustration of his readiness to aid in everything that should benefit the institution, Professor Silliman records in his diary that, when in 1810 the valuable cabinet of minerals belonging to the late Col. Gibbs was offered to the college to be kept there, if the authorities would provide suitable rooms for it, he "lost no time in laying the subject before President Dwight," and, he adds, that he "warmly espoused the design, and, without hesitation, acceded to the plan which was suggested." For the effecting of these objects and the enlargement of the means of instruction he contributed liberally himself, for it is said that, though entitled by vote of the corporation as well as by the justice of the case to the salaries of the two offices which he held, namely, that of President and that of Professor of Divinity, he regularly relinquished from one half to two thirds of what he would properly have received from the professorship. "The amount thus relinquished was more than ten thousand dollars." He also declined any increase of his salary as president, though it was offered him during the last thirteen years of his official life. That he was a devoted and generous friend of the college, as well as a wise worker for its well being, is manifested by this fact, for he was a man of only moderate means, and at his death he left his family with a limited property. It has been one of the fortunate things in the history of Yale College, that it has had within the circle of its faculty more than one who, like this eminent man, has contributed liberally of his own means for its success and growth. Indeed, the whole-souled consecration of its officers to its interests of every kind has been one of the greatest sources of its prosperity in the past, and it is most earnestly to be desired that the same spirit may characterize those who shall guide its course in the generations to come.

In regard to discipline in the college, President Dwight seems, from the very beginning of his official life, to have determined upon a thorough and radical change from the system known in earlier years. With an abounding common sense and an appreciation of the altered circumstances of the times, he removed from the college laws the old regulations respecting fines for absence from appointed exercises, and those provisions which placed the lower classes in a kind of subjection to the higher. In place of these disciplinary methods he introduced others which were more adapted to the government of a body of young men in a course of education. Especially he relied, so far as his own relations to the students were concerned, upon his personal power and influence. "No person," says the late Professor Kingsley, "ever more thoroughly understood the feelings and passions of young men, and their modes of thinking and reasoning, or knew better what motives to urge when it was necessary to check their waywardness or to incite them to laudable efforts. Whether he had occasion to speak to the students at large, or to portions of them, he always succeeded in producing a conviction of the interest he took in their welfare, in which there was no affectation; and he addressed, at the same time, their understandings and their consciences with such appropriateness and force that few continued in opposition." Having faith in paternal rather than mere governmental discipline, he treated the students as gentlemen and as sons. Such a paternal relation was more easily sustained at that period, of course, than it could be now, for the numbers in the college were so much smaller. The successive senior classes, also, were more exclusively brought under his own care and teaching than they are at present. He was, thus, more like Dr. Arnold among his scholars at Rugby than the chief officer of a great university, in our day, is able to be. The power of his personality, therefore, on each individual could be greater. But this personal power—whether then or now—is, after all, the great thing, both in discipline and in education ; and he had the keen mental perception to recognize this fact, as well as the rare faculty of using his personal influence with success upon all classes of students. The consequence was that he attached them to himself and made them his affectionate friends. "The anxiety of President Dwight for the good of his pupils," says Professor Silliman, "did not cease with the cessation of his authority over them. He was often known to converse, in the kindest and most paternal manner, with those who, having received the honors of the institution, were about to go out into the world, but concerning whose welfare he was still solicitous; and such advice, unattended by any academic sanctions, was found in various instances precious to him who was the subject of it." "The great secret of his government was this," says the same gentleman, "it was a sway of influence rather than of coercion." He was a disciplinarian, accordingly, of the highest order, for he exercised discipline without the show of it, and moved the hearts of his pupils like a loving father.

As an instructor, he had that most valuable gift which we may call magnetic power. He not only imparted knowledge to the students, and presented truth with great clearness before their minds, but he both stimulated them to activity in the independent search after truth for themselves and inspired them with enthusiasm in their work. The young man who goes forth from his college life having his mind crowded with the facts of science or of history, or with the grammar or vocabulary of the ancient languages stored in his memory— however much he may know—gives no such grand promise of the future as he who has learned to love knowledge for its own sake, and has had awakened within him an unquenchable desire to attain it. The arousing of the pupil's mind into a self-propelling activity is the most desirable end in education. It is, also, the one most difficult to be secured; and it is a grievous thing, which we are obliged to confess, that the teachers who know the secret of its accomplishment are only here and there to be found. But if there is any point on which all the graduates of Yale College under Dr. Dwight's administration are harmonious in their declarations, it is that he was such a stimulating teacher. As the late Dr. Gardiner Spring said to the alumni of the college in New York, in 1817, "There is one spot to which you will never turn your thoughts without the recollection of his full-orbed excellence, namely, the recitation room of the Senior Class. I am persuaded that I shall ever account it one of the highest privileges of my life, that my youthful allotment was to listen to the instructions of that memorable chamber."

From the accounts given of him by some of the leading men who were his pupils, however, it is clear that he was a lecturer rather than a hearer of recitations; that he aimed in the class room rather to impart knowledge to the mind of the student than to draw knowledge out of it. It could scarcely have been otherwise with a man who had such varied information, and, at the same time, so irresistible an impulse to communicate to others his own ideas and thoughts. Under the influence of such a teacher, those who are incapable of enthusiasm, or who are determined to neglect their opportunities and waste their time, may, perhaps, be carried forward less successfully than if they were forced to learn according to some dry routine or machine-like system. But even if this be true, the number in his case who resisted the magnetic influence was very small, while the gain for those who were borne along by its quickening power far more than compensated for the losses of such thoughtless and sluggish minds. The young men who were inspired by him, as one of them has said, " found their sum of knowledge daily increased; their moral principles formed and strengthened; from boys they became men, and rose to the full consciousness of manhood." I cannot forbear to add, from the testimony of this same person—Professor Denison Olmsted —who came under his instructions when he was at the very height of his power, a brief description, which will picture him before our minds in a life-like way.

" Copious and able as were the instructions given by President Dwight, in connection with the text books," Professor Olmsted says: " it was in the ample and profound discussions of questions, whether philosophical, political, literary or religious, that his great powers as a teacher were most fully brought out. In these, according to the nature of the subject, appeared, by turns, the divine, the poet, the statesman, the patriot, the philanthropist. He would enter with all his soul into the discussion, bringing forward in luminous order the most convincing arguments, embellishing by rhetorical figures, illustrating by pertinent anecdotes, enlivening by sallies of humor, and often warming up into a more glowing strain of eloquence than he ever exemplified in his public discourses. During the reading of the debates of the students he often interspersed remarks suggested by some casual association, which led him at a distance from the main point in argument. But it was useful information, however discursive he might sometimes appear; and, by this practice, he touched upon so many of the exigencies of real life that his pupils have been often heard to say that hardly a day of their subsequent lives passed without their recalling something said by President Dwight. The earnestness with which he engaged in the business of instruction, and in arguing questions in which important truths were to be established, never abated. It might be the twentieth or the thirtieth class of pupils now before him, and he might be reiterating the same ground for the thirtieth time, yet his zeal knew no satiety." Writing soon after the death of Dr. Dwight, the same distinguished gentleman said, " Who has ever united in a higher degree the dignity that commands respect, the accuracy that inspires confidence, the ardor that kindles animation, the kindness that wins affection, and has been able at the same time to exhibit before his pupils the fruits of long and profound research, of an extensive and profitable intercourse with the world, and of great experience in the business of instruction ?" This was a judgment pronounced when the writer of the words was a young graduate of only four years' standing. In 1858, he confirms the same judgment in the following language: "After the lapse of more than forty years, and after much opportunity with many eminent instructors, this estimate seems to me entirely just, and President Dwight is ever present to my mind as the Great Model Teacher." Truly the presence of such an instructor for twenty-two years in any institution of learning—if he does nothing beyond the work of the lecture room—is a power for good, which can only be fully measured when the results of all the lives, into which his thoughts and teachings have entered, shall be complete. But how much beyond this, as we have already seen, was accomplished for Yale College by this great and faithful man!

Dr. Dwight, however, was not only the President of the College, with the various duties which belong to that position. He was also the college preacher. The Professorship of Divinity, to which the care of the college church, both in preaching and the pastoral office, was assigned, had been vacant for two years when the new president was inaugurated. Several attempts were made by the Corporation to fill the chair, but without success, and in the meantime Dr. Dwight supplied the pulpit. At length, in 1805 it was decided to elect him to the professorship, and from that time till his death he discharged all its duties. By leaving the parish where he had been settled for twelve years, therefore, he did not cease to be a preacher or to have the spiritual oversight of a congregation. On the contrary, he entered upon a similar work to that in which he had been engaged, only in a field where he had the greatest opportunities for usefulness, and where, if successful, his Christian influence was destined to be far reaching.

The taste and peculiarities of successive generations differ in no respect more widely, perhaps, than they do with reference to preaching. The people of to-day, therefore, are unable to judge with entire fairness of the sermons which their fathers heard, or even of those which they heard themselves in their earlier life. We have a new standard, of which our ancestors knew nothing. To the audiences of his own generation Dr. Dwight was a most effective and eloquent preacher. He broke away from the dry and doctrinal method of the New England ministers who preceded him, and his sermons mark an era in that progress of preaching which has resulted in the highest and best style of our own generation. But we may say more than this. The sermons which were published after his death, and which present his system of theology, have been regarded ever since their publication, as among the ablest productions of the American pulpit. For clearness and felicity of statement, and for force and candor in dealing with objections, they are unsurpassed by any theological writings. In England, as well as in our own land, they have exerted a very wide influence, and, in the former country especially, they have been to so great a degree an element in theological education that almost all prominent English clergymen—at least those not of the Established Church—who come to our shores, bear testimony to what they themselves have owed to their author. "There may have been other preachers," says that eminent clergyman, of whose death we have just heard—the Rev. Dr. William B. Sprague—"there may have been other preachers who could occasionally rise to a loftier height and produce a more overwhelming impression than he; but, if there have been those, at least in our own country, whose ministrations were uniformly marked with more vigor and dignity and attraction than his, we know not where to look for them."

As a theologian he was not an originator or discoverer, like his ancestor the elder Edwards, or his pupil Dr. Taylor, but I suppose that no man in the history of New England, unless it be Edwards himself, has affected theological thinking in a greater degree, or done more to give theology its true place as the queen of the sciences. Dr. Dwight, however, as a theologian and as a preacher, aimed at practical results. At the beginning of his official life as president he labored most earnestly and successfully for the overthrow of the infidel ideas of the time, which had seized upon the minds of the ablest young men, and had so pervaded the college that the church had scarcely any members. His arguments and discourses on this subject were remembered long after the conflict was ended and the victory secured. But in the quieter period that followed, even to the close of his career, he preached, with all the energy of his soul, for the conversion and the religious upbuilding of the students. Revivals of much power attended his efforts. The lives of many of his pupils bore witness, in their own Christian development, to the faithfulness of his personal solicitations and his persuasive appeals. Believing in the infinite value to the soul of its union with God by a living faith, he thought that education attained its highest end only when it brought the knowledge of spiritual and eternal realities. He consecrated, therefore, all his working and all his life to the securing of such an education for the hundreds of young men who came within the sphere of his influence. "It was impossible not to love him," says the late Nathaniel Chauncey, Esq., of Philadelphia, for "his prayers and exertions and talents were constantly employed for the good of his charge; his praise, delightful as the approbation of conscience, and reproof, piercing to the soul, both alike evidently came from the feelings of a father, who taught not only how to live but how to die."

I may add that Dr. Dwight's influence did not end with what he did or what he taught. It belonged to his very nature. It had its foundation in himself. Every student who came to Yale College saw in its President a grand specimen of man. He was not greater than some other men, of that generation or of this, in particular lines; probably he was not the equal of some. But, if we may give any credence to what the fathers have told us, he was one of the most conspicuous of men in modern times for the roundness and fullness, the variety and symmetry of his powers.

He was an ardent lover of music; a poet of some merit, to say the least, considering the age; a teacher of extraordinary ability; one of the first preachers of his generation. He was acquainted with almost every subject, had read extensively in the literature of the English language, was a delighted observer of nature, loved flowers and all beautiful things with the ardor of a child, and opened his mind to be taught in everything useful, from the highest to the lowest sphere. He had practical wisdom to devise plans for needed improvements, and practical energy to carry out these plans to their result, to a degree which few have ever surpassed. He had a hopeful outlook upon the future and believed that the golden age was yet to come, and he was ready for every necessary effort and sacrifice to make that future possible, as well as to hasten its coming. He was a patriot, with the most ardent love for his country; believing in liberty and abhorring the system which brought human beings into bondage and deprived them of all their dearest rights. He was a Christian believer, of the humblest and most earnest kind; full of love for his fellow men, and ever ready to give them sympathy and help on their way to heaven. With reasoning powers of a high order, with a cultivated imagination, with a conversational ability admired by all the circle of his acquaintance, and by strangers even who met him for the first time, with the manners of a gentleman, and, in a wonderful degree, the bearing and person of a noble man—his form erect and full of dignity, his face beaming with intelligence and virtue, and his whole appearance impressive and commanding—with all this so conspicuous to every beholder, he must have filled the college with the refinement of his presence; he must have been, as they saw him from day to day, an example to all his pupils, which they could not but desire to imitate. I would that I might have seen him as he moved about among the people of Greenfield, or as he walked the quiet streets of New Haven; a generous, earnest, thoughtful, benignant Christian preacher and teacher.

It was such a man that this church, after enjoying his ministry for twelve years, gave up, at the Divine summons, for the college of this Commonwealth. More than half a century has passed since his earthly career came to its end, and more than three quarters of a century since he closed his labors here. The men whom he knew in Greenfield have all entered into the experiences of the other life, like himself. Even of those who knew him as his pupils at New Haven but a small number still survive. His wife, who came to this place with him in her early life, lived on alone in her widowhood, universally revered and beloved, till she was ninety-one, but it is now thirty years since her departure from this world; and their children, after long and useful and honored lives, have all finished their work, and are now reunited with him and with her in heaven. So the grandchildren come forward to the places of the grandfathers, and the generations move on in their ceaseless course. But like the everlasting hills, the memory of the past still abides, and we who meet on this commemorative day bless God for the great men of other times.

There is a beautiful hymn, which was written soon after the close of his ministry here, by the pastor and teacher in whose honor I have spoken—a hymn sung by sweet voices all over the English-speaking world, and destined to be sung more and more widely to the latest time—a true song of the Church, which will give expression to the sentiment of thousands of the great brotherhood of believers, who will never know of the life of its author. As I hold it in my hand at this moment, in the old manuscript where he wrote its words, and as the passing of these hundred and fifty years in this village church brings to our thoughts the faithfulness of God in the past and His promises for the future, it seems almost as if he stood upon this sacred spot once more, and, with all the ardor of his Christian confidence and hope, said, as he did so long ago:

I love thy kingdom, Lord,
　The house of thine abode,
The church our blest Redeemer saved
　With his own precious blood.

I love thy church. O God!
　Her walls before thee stand,
Dear as the apple of thine eye,
　And graven on thy hand.

If e'er to bless thy sons
　My voice or hands deny,
These hands let useful skill forsake
　This voice in silence die.

If e'er my heart forget
　Her welfare or her woe,
Let every joy this heart forsake
　And every grief o'erflow.

For her my tears shall fall,
　For her my prayers ascend,
To her my cares and toils be given
　'Till toils and cares shall end.

Beyond my highest joy
　I prize her heavenly ways,
Her sweet communion, solemn vows,
　Her hymns of love and praise.

Jesus, thou Prince divine,
　Our Saviour and our King,
Thy hand from every snare and foe
　Shall great deliverance bring.

Sure as thy truth shall last,
　To Zion shall be given
The brightest glories earth can yield,
　And brighter bliss of heaven.

www.ingramcontent.com/pod-product-compliance
Lightning Source LLC
Chambersburg PA
CBHW030015030726
47499CB00008B/3012